TABOO & TRANSCENDING Tales

OF HISTORICAL SCI-FI & FANTASY

RICH DISILVIO

- - - - - - - - - - - - - - - - -

Names: DiSilvio, Rich
Title: Taboo & Transcending Tales of Historical Sci-Fi & Fantasy / Rich DiSilvio
Description: New York, USA: DV Books, an imprint of Digital Vista, inc.
Identifiers: 978-1-950052-17-2 (paperback) |
ISBN 978-1-950052-16-5 (eBook)
Subjects: Short Stories | Sci-Fi | Fantasy | Science Fiction | History | Religion
Illustrations/Photos: 12

Special Note About This Book

The fact that some of the world's greatest thinkers didn't believe in Jesus or God gives us pause to consider their perspectives. Men like Thomas Jefferson, Benjamin Franklin, James Madison, Thomas Paine, Voltaire and Ethan Allen were all Deists, believing in an unknown Creator of Nature, while brilliant scientists and thinkers like Albert Einstein, Carl Sagan, David Hume, Richard Dawkins, Christopher Hitchens, Stephen Hawking, Linus Pauling, Francis Crick, Charles Darwin, Bertrand Russell and Richard Feynman were Atheists or Deists.

Naturally this is only a partial list, but that many great minds have given serious thought to this critical subject, one that has inculcated the majority of people for thousands of years and governs their lives in profound ways, is a topic worthy of closer reevaluation. While some of the tales herein praise God and the status quo, others question our belief systems and offer food for thought. This topic, which is taboo in most circles today, is here to expose both sides, and may the reader decide for his or her own self. At a bare minimum, I hope that infusing such profound thoughts into fictional tales at least offers entertainment for all to enjoy.

Contents

THE AURA OF ST. FRANCIS

In the heart of Rome, the eminent Hungarian composer Franz Liszt sat at his piano working on the sheet music for his latest work entitled *St. Francis of Assisi Preaching to the Birds*. Just outside his window was his inspiration, a new statue of St. Francis in the nearby plaza.

A small grotto of grapevines had been built behind the saint with a wooden table in front of him. The sculptor had placed a bowl of grapes on the table days ago in an effort to attract birds to enliven his sculptural display to gain attention. Yet not a single bird appeared. For the saintly work of art hadn't elicited any interest or praise he was hoping for, and Mayor Leopoldo Torlonia was making another visit today to inspect the results.

The mayor walked up and rolled his eyes. Once again, he noticed that no one even looked at the statue as they went about their business, unaware of the investment he authorized on behalf of the Eternal City. With a huff, he turned and, unexpectedly, spotted Liszt gazing out the widow of his residence. He nodded a greeting, to which Liszt waved for him to come over.

As the mayor walked over, Liszt opened the door. "Good day, Mayor Torlonia! I have seen you several times over the past few weeks gazing at the statue. It is truly a magnificent work of a worthy subject, is it not?"

The mayor took off his hat as he entered Liszt's residence and replied with a scowl, "I regret to be the bearer of bad news, Maestro, but it is scheduled to be demolished. I plan to replace it with a water fountain. Something the people always find alluring and stimulating. You know, something with *action*."

Liszt's gracious face withered to a solemn stare. "I truly hope you're not serious?" He turned to look out the window again at the saintly statue standing amid a wholesome grotto. "It's simply divine, mayor. What is not to love about it? Just because it's devoid of movement doesn't mean it's devoid of artistic and spiritual merit. The *Mona Lisa* does not move, but she smiles upon the world, who in turn smiles upon her… and will for all eternity."

Mayor Torlonia stood firm, ironically like the statue, and declared, "I value great art like the next man, Maestro, but I'm a politician, and I must keep my constituents happy. Otherwise my mayoral career will be *demolished*, rather than that statue." He glanced out the window at the static statue, and continued, "That chunk of marble stood there for over three weeks without a single response by the public. It appears Saint Francis evidently has no more influence. Even his cherished birds refused to honor it with their presence or even anoint it with their feces. That's how uneventful it is. It must go!"

Liszt sighed and pointed to a chair near his piano. "Please, have a seat. Allow me to show you how one creation inspires another, even in a different art form. For that statue gave me the inspiration to write my latest piece, entitled *St. Francis of Assisi Preaching to the Birds*. So that statue already fulfilled a noble purpose."

The mayor slapped his hat against his thigh. "Very well, Maestro. Let me hear this song of yours." With that, he reluctantly complied, sitting with his hat on his lap and his chin resting on his knuckles.

Liszt sat down at the piano and organized the loose sheets he had written thus far. He then threw back his head and longhair, looking up at the heavens through the ceiling, and took a deep breath. Summoning a state of utter tranquility, he then drew the essence of Saint Francis into his very soul, as he lowered his head and softly played the first few pages of the unfinished composition.

Being the ultimate pioneer of his age, Liszt had always been a trailblazer. As such, his peers often misunderstood him, which was to be expected, as Liszt's music was often a century ahead of its time.

The mayor sat gazing emptily at the floor, until he realized the music had stopped. Awkwardly, he looked up. "My apologies, Maestro. I adore many of your older pieces, especially your *Liebestraume* or *Un Sospiro*. But *this*, well; this just doesn't make much sense to me as 'music.' I really don't know how to even describe it."

Liszt nodded, well aware of the common refrains from common people. "Don't think of it as a traditional song, with a pretty melody," Liszt said. "Think of it in your mind and envision St. Francis lovingly interacting with the birds, they chirping and he blessing them with a hymn."

The mayor rolled his eyes. "I'm sorry, but this new type of music *is* for the birds! So, pardon me for being so abrupt, but…" He stood up and started to walk toward the door. "My mind is made up. Tomorrow the statue *will* be demolished!"

Liszt sprung up and followed him to the door. "But what if a miracle occurs, Mayor? Would you change your bird-brained verdict then?"

The mayor frowned as he abruptly stopped and spun around. But then his scowl flipped and he chuckled, relishing Liszt's quick wit, by hurling the bird insult right back at him. He recalled how Liszt would scold even royalty if they demeaned him or his work in any fashion, and the mayor admired Liszt's devotion to high art and his fierce integrity. "Very well, Master Liszt. If God somehow gives us a sign, I'll bow to your and His will."

With that, the mayor left, as Liszt closed the door. With a sigh of disappointment and only a glimmer of hope, he resumed composing his saintly piece of music. After an hour of romancing the keys and scribbling notes on paper, Liszt lit a cigar and took several puffs. His eyelids grew heavy. He walked over to the console and poured himself a glass of cognac. Downing the charge in one hefty gulp, he licked his lips. He then sat down, leaned back and closed his eyes. The seconds turned to minutes and he soon slipped into a deep, dark slumber, when his mind mysteriously awakened to a distant and vivid dream.

Standing in the port city of Damietta, Egypt was Francis of Assisi and one of his devout followers, Illuminatus of Arce.

It was 1219, and the Fifth Crusade was in its second year of struggle to recapture the Holy Land from the Muslims. On orders from Pope Innocent III, several European monarchs had been convinced that another Crusade was critical, not only to rectify the disastrous loss of the Fourth Crusade, but also to push back the advances of the Islamic invaders who had conquered so much of the

Catholic kingdom. Moreover, the Muslim's intense intolerance, as instructed in their *Quran*, had put targets on the backs of every Christian, being lethally condemned as infidels to Allah.

Weeks earlier, the Crusaders had launched an attack on the Tower of Damietta, which sat imposingly on the edge of the Nile River and was heavily fortified with Islamic soldiers. Moreover, it featured a huge chain that spanned the river, thus preventing enemy ships from gaining access inland. The first attempt to breach the fortress had failed, but they later managed to break through with a miraculous victory. Adding to the heralded triumph was news several days later that Sultan al-Adil had died.

Pelagius, *papal legate* and self-proclaimed commander of the Crusade, had then attempted to push upriver with a huge raft, but suffered a devastating loss.

On the riverbank, Francis and Illuminatus approached the commander. Francis introduced himself and his follower, while Pelagius eyed Francis from head to toe with little enthusiasm. In fact, he was well acquainted with the passive nature of the friar's reputation, of loving every creature on Earth, and even chatting with silly birds.

Nevertheless, Francis made his plea. "Commander Pelagius, despite our providential victory of seizing the port and news of the sultan's death, the current setback has us at a impasse. As such, Illuminatus and I appeal to your good judgment to allow us to have an audience with the dead sultan's son, al-Kamil."

Pelagius sniggered as he slapped his sword against his leg. "Do you have a death wish, Francis? As you said, they have suffered a loss and his father is dead. I'm quite certain that a grieving son will have little to no sympathy for you or any Christian."

"But they already reached out and offered us a settlement," Francis said with expectation, yet he added with regret, "One that I hear you plan to refuse."

"And well I should refuse!" Pelagius blustered. "I am ordained by the pope to defend our rightful honor and glory after our disastrous defeat with the last Crusade. Therefore, my plan is to annihilate these heretics, who have the audacity to call *us* infidels! Do I make myself clear?"

As Crusaders scurried to and fro, setting up camp, Francis took a deep breath. "But the new sultan, al-Kamil, has sensibly offered to give us back the Holy Land if we retreat from Egypt. That seems quite reasonable to me. It would give us what we set out to do and would eliminate many unnecessary deaths."

"Reasonable to *you*," Pelagius retorted. "But not to *me*. I thought you, a friar, with your new flock of followers, would appreciate men like me, for not just aiming to recoup our Holy Land, but for quashing evil savages like these Muslims who have grown more hostile ever since their militant messiah started their cult. Hasn't the Lord given you divine vision? Can't you see that a growing army of idol-worshipping demons is threatening the very existence of Christendom? As passive as you and your followers are, friar, this contagion is something you must acknowledge and it must be annihilated!" Pelagius groaned with humiliation. Taking a breath, he regained his composure, then added calmly, "And what exactly do wish to accomplish by having a meeting with the new sultan?"

Francis glanced at Illuminatus then back at Pelagius. "I am convinced that the Lord will oversee my actions, and that is to convince the sultan of their misguided ways and convert him to the true light of the world, Jesus Christ."

Pelagius looked sideways, and burst out laughing. Sliding his sword back into its scabbard, he turned back and retorted sardonically, "Francis, you might as well preach to your silly birds, because you'll get the same useless response from that evil ruler. Correction, his demonic chirp will be to his executioner, who will fillet you, and then serve you up like a roasted duck!"

As several Crusaders nearby heard their leader's remark they all laughed. Francis looked at Illuminatus solemnly with great reserve, not embarrassed nor broken, but sad at Pelagius' blindness to the Lord's will and power. He looked back at Pelagius. "Then you have nothing to lose, Commander, for it is only I who faces death if unsuccessful. And al-Kamil has offered peace, yet you refused. Therefore, I believe he will be more open-minded and conciliatory to a *Higher* appeal."

Pelagius smirked at the subtle slur, and was about to reprimand the insolent friar, but then shook his head. "Very well, Francis. Do what you like. I will shake your hand to bid you farewell, so I can tell the pope when I return victorious, without your presence, that I at least had the good fortune to shake your hallowed hand before your demise."

Francis ignored the insult and the handshake, and just turned around and marched away, saying, "Thank you, Commander," as Illuminatus devoutly followed suit.

Francis and Illuminatus journeyed across the military border and were granted an audience with Sultan al-Kamil, who greeted them warmly. As Francis expected, the sultan was more responsive and amiable than Pelagius believed, and listened to him preach the Word of the Lord without malice of heart or blind ignorance. However, al-Kamil, whether firm in his Islamic faith or fearful that openly abandoning Muhammad to embrace Jesus would secure his death, politely refused to convert. Nevertheless, he generously granted Francis permission to preach freely in the Holy Land, of which he still had possession.

Francis left peacefully and continued his ministry for years. Yet, as fate would have it, Francis was vindicated twenty years after he died when al-Kamil asked to be baptized on his deathbed.

With a loud bang on the door, Franz Liszt woke up, startled and disoriented. He blinked hard. *Dear Lord!* He thought. *Where am I?*

As the knocking on the door persisted, Liszt rose to his feet and walked over to open the door. There stood Mayor Torlonia. "It seems you got your way, Maestro."

Still disoriented and contemplating his daydream, Liszt squinted. "Got my way with what, exactly?"

"Look out your window."

Liszt turned and gazed out, when suddenly his eyes enlarged with glee! Fluttering all around the statue of Saint Francis was a flock of vivacious birds, all of various species and vibrant colors. With a beam of sun shinning on the statue, it truly was a spectacle of sublime divination, as citizens and tourists flocked to see the luminous statue, as if it were orchestrating the aerial acrobatics of adoration.

A delightful grin enlivened Liszt's face with utter grace. He gazed back at the mayor. "Yes, I may have gotten my way, Mayor Torlonia, but it was a joint effort by us two Francises and the good Lord above."

The mayor laughed, just now realizing that the name *Franz* was also derived from the same Latin root as *Francis*. "Yes, your Trinity has prevailed, Maestro Liszt. The statue shall remain."

Adam's Atom

The ungodly frigid cold of Antarctica numbed the faces of Evelyn and Sadam as they made their way across the frozen tundra. Riding on the back of a huge dog sled loaded with supplies, the newlyweds sought shelter. The year was 2050 and they were devastated by the unimaginable thought that the rest of planet Earth was a wasteland. They were the proverbial sole survivors of the human race.

Evidently mankind wasn't so kind, as they had polluted every aspect of Earth's nurturing crust, from its once fertile plains and rainforests to its once pristine waters, to its once pure air, right down to her plate tectonics that they unwittingly blasted with hydrogen bomb tests that destroyed its integrity and radiated countless miles of geography. And to top it off, Russia, China, North Korea, England, India, and the United States offered the final deathblow that had forced Evelyn and Sadam to flee two weeks before Armageddon to reach Antarctica.

Now left in the unbearable terrain of ice, snow, and frigid waters, the couple pushed forward with a loaded sled hauled by a team of twelve dogs. They knew they had to find shelter fast as the South Pole only offered four hours of daylight. Worse yet, they could see an ominous snowstorm on the dark horizon.

Evelyn was understandably at her wit's end over the traumatic events, as a tear froze on her alabaster cheek. She looked at Sadam, with his tan skin, black hair and frozen goatee. "This is useless. We'll never survive in this climate, and God knows when or if we'll ever be able to return north to the warm, southern shores of Australia or Africa."

Sadam shook his head with a frown. "Evelyn, we know the rest of the planet is heavily polluted and toxic with radiation. And our boat was badly damaged by the ice. We were lucky we even reached land. So, we can't think of heading north. We must focus on survival, *here*." He cracked the whip in the air to accelerate the huskies, which obediently responded.

Aiming to lift his wife's spirits, he called out, "On Dasher, on Prancer, on Donna, and Blitzen!"

Achieving his objective, Evelyn looked at him and chuckled. "You're an idiot. This is not funny, Sadam Santa."

Sadam smiled. "No, it's not. But levity is the best medicine for depression."

"We'll, thanks for the amusing tonic, but how much longer can we survive down here in this outdoor freezer?"

Sadam's eyes lit up. "Maybe longer than you think!"

"What do you mean?"

"Look over there," he said, pointing to a large wooden structure sticking halfway out of the snow.

"What do you suppose it is?" She replied, equally curious.

"Not sure," he said. "But it definitely is a sign of life, human life."

As he steered the sled toward the structure, she replied, "But I don't see any life, just dead wood."

As they approached, he said, "That's not just dead wood, Evelyn. That's part of an old ship."

Stopping the sled, they each hopped off and walked over to the battered structure. Sadam smiled as he looked at the word printed on it. "It's the stern of *Endurance*!"

Evelyn squinted. "I no longer have much endurance, but what is this?"

Sadam gazed in wonder at the remnants of the tail end of the ship, which housed the captain's cabin. "That's why we need to read history more often, Evelyn. All I recall is that *Endurance* was the ship Ernest Shackleton and his crew used to explore Antarctica, I think from 1914 to 1917 or 18."

Evelyn nodded tepidly as her teeth chattered. "Oh, yes, I vaguely recall his name," she said, as she rubbed her biceps briskly to warm herself. "But wait..." she added. "They never returned. They all..." she stammered, then added fretfully, "Died."

"Yes, I think so," he said, not recalling every detail. "But I do know that the *Endurance* was supposed to have sunk." His eyes scanned the slanted structure. "Yet, evidently her stern broke free from the rest of the ship and managed to stay frozen in the ice."

Eagerly, he crawled inside the cabin and quickly assessed its stability. He popped his head back out. "This is a gift from Allah, Evelyn! This cabin is suitable for shelter."

Evelyn tried to smile but couldn't. "Well, I believe it was a gift from Jesus, but either way, that will not be sufficient to keep us warm for long, sweetheart."

"Oh, stop being a defeatist, Evelyn," he scolded, as he quickly started to unload the suitcases and containers of food off the sled. "Come on!" he urged fretfully as he glanced back at the rapidly approaching blizzard. "We don't have much time."

"Not much time, indeed," she moaned. "That's the understatement of all mankind."

As her eyes caught a glimpse of the ominous storm, Evelyn jumped with urgency and assisted Sadam with the cargo. Then they unleashed the dogs and brought them into the cabin, where they locked down and braced themselves for the storm.

With massive force, the blizzard battered the old, rickety cabin, as small, loose planks tore off and the wind whistled and howled. The huskies responded in kind to the howls, driving Sadam and Evelyn a bit mad, yet they knew without Shackleton's cabin they would have all been dead.

Sadam rummaged through some cabinets and drawers and came upon an old newspaper. His head sprung up. "Hey, get a load of this! Shackleton had posted an advertisement in this London paper, stating: 'Men wanted for hazardous journey. Low wages, bitter cold, long hours of complete darkness. Safe return doubtful. Honor and recognition in the event of success.'" He looked at Evelyn.

"Isn't that a crazy advertisement? Who in their right mind would respond to such a frightening ad like that?"

"And here we are," Evelyn moaned as she opened a can of fruit.

"Hey, come on," Sadam said. "We didn't elect to come here. Allah, or Jesus, or whomever, ordained this, for some unknown reason. After all, Noah survived the Great Flood. So it seems we've been chosen, as well."

"Chosen is the wrong word, Sadam. It's more like condemned."

Sadam shook his head. He realized nothing he could ever say would be met with enthusiasm or even the slightest bit of hope. He resumed rummaging through the drawers when he came upon another amazing find; a bundle of old black and white photos.

Sadam's eyes widened with wonder at the historic photos of Shackleton and his crew. Slowly he slid one photo out of the bundle after another, sliding the viewed ones at the bottom of the stack. "Look at this, they took some amazing shots, Evelyn."

Evelyn just sat eating peaches and cherries on a broken bench, as she gazed emptily at the wooden floorboards. She barely acknowledged him with a nod.

Meanwhile, Sadam slid one photo after another, until his eyes bulged with shock! "Dear God! What the hell is *this*!?"

His reaction finally stirred Evelyn to at least lift her head. "What is it?"

Sadam was momentarily speechless as he stared unnervingly at the chilling photo. Swallowing a lump of dread, he uttered, "It's some type of colossal ice sculpture. It's the size of a thirty-story building... of... an... ugly creature's head."

Evelyn squinted, then laughed. "You must be kidding? What kind of snow creature would the Shackleton crew make, an ugly mermaid?"

"No. Come and look at this," he said, still half dazed.

Evelyn walked over and was immediately thunderstruck, as well. "Dear Lord! What a hideous thing to make." She blinked hard. "Why would Shackleton and his crew waste precious time making something so gargantuan and time consuming as this?"

With his mind now clear, Sadam said, "There's no way they did this. As you say, they were struggling just to survive and failed at that. This was made by, well, it could only have been made by… something else."

Evelyn drew in a huge and uncomfortable breath. "You can't be serious? *Aliens?*"

"What else could have done this?" he said. "Or would have done this, if not another life form? The sheer scale of this monumental alien head is also quite disturbing. If this is a life-sized bust, these aliens are giants."

"Well, we Americans built Mount Rushmore, and the Indians built that gargantuan statue of Vallabhbhai Patel."

Sadam nodded with a bit of relief. "Yes, that's true. The Patel statue was almost 600 feet tall and made of bronze and steel." He gazed back down at the disturbing photo. Something this enormous must still remain, at least in part. It has to be somewhere nearby if Shackleton took these photos." He looked at Evelyn. "Tomorrow we'll start our search."

Hours later the blizzard subsided and the two survivors and their canine team managed to fall asleep for eleven hours. With the extended darkness, they didn't even realize they had slept so long. Nevertheless, they readied the sled and dogs, and set out across the frozen tundra in search of the colossal ice sculpture.

Cracking the whip and yelling to his team, Sadam motivated the canines to trample through the snow, as Evelyn wrapped a scarf around her freezing face. Over snowdrifts and past cracked ice sheets they rode for an hour, when she spotted something in the distance. "Look! Over there," she said, pointing to her right. "That looks like something, doesn't it?"

"Indeed, it does," Sadam replied, as he steered the huskies toward the large snow-covered mountain with what appeared to be a cave entrance. Coming to a stop, they both hopped off and walked toward the small opening at the bottom of the huge vertical wall of snow. It was clear that it was the lower portion of the alien head sculpture they had seen in the photo. However, it was only the neck with a cave entrance carved into it, which went deep into the mountain. They entered the ice cave and walked several yards in, when suddenly they gasped!

They looked at each other, as an internal chill rippled their skin. Up ahead they could see a shiny metal door.

Evelyn muttered, "Jesus, you don't think they're still here, do you?"

Sadam bit his lip. "I pray to Allah they're not."

Shattering their nerves, the door slowly opened!

Evelyn grabbed Sadam's arm. "Oh, no! no! no! no," she whimpered, as a strange ungodly creature emerged from the ice cave, with four others standing right behind.

Sadam couldn't believe his eyes as the foremost creature waved for them to proceed forth with an awkward yet amicable smile. They all appeared to be about seven feet tall and had huge heads with black eyes and skinny arms; while all five wore the same drab gray one-piece suits with black boots.

Sadam whispered, "Well, thank goodness they're not the mega giants I feared. But, if we run, I'm sure these things, with such long and strong legs like that, will catch us. So perhaps we should comply."

Evelyn squeezed his arm even tighter. "I don't know about that. We do have a team of dogs."

Just then, the lead creature called out in English. "Don't be afraid. We mean you no harm. You'll be pleased to know that we've been here far longer than you humans, on the order of a few million years. Please proceed."

Evelyn rolled her eyes. "A few million years?" she whispered. "They're lying already. And I'll bet they destroyed Shackleton's ship and killed his crew. Let's go!"

Sadam sighed, as he looked deep into her sapphire blue eyes. "You've been the one always throwing in the towel. So, if you truly believe we have no chance of surviving, there's nothing to lose by accepting their invitation."

Evelyn now looked deep into Sadam's vibrant brown eyes, as her tight grip loosened. "I guess you're right," she loathed admitting. "And at least they speak English. So, let's see who they *really* are."

With that, they both walked toward the creatures. Arriving right before them, Sadam said, "Well, we're glad you speak English. Just don't say you came here to serve man."

Alidore, the prominent alien, squinted, then chuckled. "Ah, yes, I believe you're making reference to a Twilight Zone episode. Is that correct?"

Sadam was shocked, as his head snapped backward. "Oh, come on! How do you know about an old TV show?"

Alidore smiled. "As I said, the five of us have been here for millions of years and have witnessed a great deal of human evolution. And besides knowing all of your languages, we even picked up on some of your artistic and athletic pastimes, many of which are rather unimpressive. In fact, we don't understand the affinity for investing countless hours and years watching men play with a ball. However, in this case, that program at least demonstrated a high degree of intelligence and the skills for creativity."

"Wait!" Sadam exclaimed, as his mind had fixated on the alien's very first sentence. "You don't mean to tell me that you five have *personally* lived for millions of years, are you?"

"I'm afraid so," Alidore said. "Look, there's much to discuss, and I know your frail human bodies can't manage the cold, so come inside. We have several rooms that we can adjust the temperature to suit your biological infirmities."

Sadam looked at Evelyn who was shivering. "Infirmities indeed. What do you say?"

"We went this far," she said, as she feverishly rubbed her cold mittens together. "And some heat would be very much welcomed."

With that, as the couple entered, Alidore's forehead twitched, thereby making the huge alien-head sculpture reappear on the mountain. The illusion of just a mountain cliff of snow had been created with the intent of evading satellite recognition. Yet Sadam and Evelyn's on-the-ground search, based on Shackleton's vivid photos, allowed them to decipher the random snow cave entrance as being in the neck, or at least a partial neck, of the colossal alien sculpture. That Alidore's startling feat was televised on a monitor in the corridor, Sadam and Evelyn both gasped.

Bewildered, Sadam stopped, and said, "How did you, I mean...I'm guessing you have some type of mental telepathy, right?"

Alidore smiled as he waved for them to continue walking further inside the underground complex. "Well, yes, it's quite a bit more than just mental telepathy, but that's what you humans call it. We can operate and alter many things that way, and have abilities that your kind would consider, well, actually godlike."

Evelyn twisted her lips. "The only god is Jesus Christ. And that's something I've been telling Sadam for the past year we've been married."

"And I've been telling *her* its Allah well before that."

Alidore's amicable face withered to a solemn stare. "I think it's best if we all have a seat in our conference room, it is just up ahead to our left."

As they continued walking, Evelyn asked, "So, your colossal snow sculpture of a head, who is that?"

Jasidore glanced her way and said, "That is Ultradore. He has lived longer than any of us and is responsible for learning about the hidden powers our species possess and making them manifest. Our planet and species were named after him, so he is very much revered."

Alidore added, "Yes, Jasidore also happens to be Ultradore's daughter."

Evelyn looked at her. "So you must be pretty special."

Jasidore chuckled. "No. I am just one of a million."

Evelyn and Sadam looked at each other and shrugged at the odd response, as they all entered the large room. The décor was austere yet comfortable at 72 degrees, and they each took their seats around a large round table. Alidore officially introduced his cadre of four Ultradorians; namely Masidore, Jasidore, Lasidore and Casidore. The Ultradorians each mentally adjusted their thermal suits to 38 degrees, then Alidore twitched his forehead as a tray of food and drinks rose up from the center of the table.

"Please, have a cup of coffee and a sandwich. I prepared roast beef, salami, Swiss cheese, chicken, pork, as well as some vegetables and other items you humans enjoy, including even peanut butter and jelly." He looked at Sadam. "I do know Muslims do not eat pork, but feel free to partake in these other fine meats, which have all been prepared to meet your Halal requirements."

Sadam smiled. "That's truly impressive. I mean, this smorgasbord of our foods, and even knowing about the dietary requirements of Muslims." He glanced at Evelyn lovingly. "Yet, being married to a Christian, I abandoned those dietary rituals." Eagerly he grasped several different meats and placed them on rye bread with some mustard. "This is simply fantastic, we can't thank you enough."

Evelyn opted for a hot cup of coffee and peanut butter and jelly on white bread, as she cautiously bit into the sandwich.

Alidore noticed and laughed. "Fear not, Evelyn. Ultradorians have no reason to harm, or worse yet, kill you."

Calidore leaned forward and added, "Yes, remember, you humans are the killers. After all, you even wiped out your entire planet."

Evelyn and Sadam both stopped chewing, glanced at each other, then curiously looked at Calidore, then back at Alidore, as Sadam queried, "Yes, what exactly have you been doing here all these years? And if millions of years is true, why haven't you done something to save humanity, rather than just giving its last two survivors a beautiful banquet of food?"

"Please, first things first," Alidore said. "Enjoy your sandwiches and relax. We have much to tell you, and it won't be easy for you at first to believe the things we'll present. But know this, as I said already, we have no intentions of harming you. I just hope eating some food will give you both more energy and clarity of mind to hear the monumental revelations we shall impart."

Evelyn resumed chewing, slowly. Then she swallowed the nervous lump of dread and food, and asked, "If you know so much about us, you surely know that teasing us with a *monumental* statement like that does not make us comfortable. My stomach is already getting queasy."

"I can understand your anxiety," Alidore said. "In that case, I shall commence." His forehead twitched and a large screen descended from the ceiling. What appeared startled Sadam and Evelyn, as she said, "That's not what I was expecting?"

Alidore nodded. "Yes, but it's best that we start from the beginning. And that happened to be when we first arrived on this planet."

Sadam still had a hard time processing all of this, as he scoffed. "So you all *personally* arrived here millions of years ago when dinosaurs roamed the Earth?"

"Yes, I'm afraid so," Alidore said with a straight face. "I'm sure our ages shock and bewilder you, but think of it this way; your Dolania Mayfly only lives for *five minutes*. Now, compare that to the average lifespan of humans, which is about 80 years, and that equates to over *forty-two million minutes*. The difference *is* staggering. Is it not?"

Sadam's head recoiled as he contemplated that equally bewildering fact, while Evelyn interjected, "Okay, I'll play along. So you're millions of years old. But why did you come here? Did you all screw up and destroy your planet like we did ours?"

Alidore smiled thoughtfully. "No, my dear. Never would we do such a foolish thing. Sadly, that's a very human trait."

"So, why Earth?" Sadam pressed, also disturbed by the insult of his entire species.

"Because we five are what you human's call scientists, or more specifically biologists. And this was the boldest project my people ever attempted."

Sadam's lips twisted. "A pet project that you invested millions of years on. Come on?"

"I told you both that this would be extremely difficult for you to understand. Your entire lives, and the billions of humans before you, have all been a project. Our biological experiment."

"And why would you do that?" Evelyn asked, now utterly humiliated. "So, we're just lab rats that you tossed into a global environment? For what purpose?"

"To expand our own mental horizons," Alidore said. "We are a species that strives to learn all the secrets and truths of the universe. And we have much to learn about the behaviors of other biological species. So, don't take this so personally. Your planet's unique animals and plants were also a significant part of this experiment. You see, when we arrived here, we observed the dinosaurs for only two hundred years or so. That was when, by chance, meteors disrupted this planet's atmosphere and climate, along with wiping out the dinosaurs."

Sadam gazed up at the large screen, as meteors burned through the atmosphere, crashing into the Earth with great force. Huge dust clouds enveloped the planet and, as the scene advanced at a fast pace, the dust settled, only to reveal millions of dead dinosaurs strewn across the planet. Advancing quickly, the scenes changed rapidly as different prehistoric eras evolved to a point where there was a close up of a picturesque landscape. Amid the lush garden of trees and vibrant flowers was a large metallic sphere with chrome strands radiating around it, looking like a huge metallic atom.

"What's that?" Sadam inquired.

Alidore looked at the screen. "That is Adam's atom. Our first capsule for the biological specimen we created. The second capsule was deployed soon after."

Sadam and Evelyn squinted, as Sadam asked, "You are kidding me, right?"

Evelyn added, "You're not going to tell us that you're God, are you?"

"I told you both that this would be extremely difficult for you to process, but in a human sense, yes. At least according to your primitive beliefs. We don't consider ourselves as gods, mind you. That's a label your ancient ancestors contrived. And that mere handful of mythmakers polluted the minds of billions of humans ever since, just because you were too lazy to truly investigate their scriptures and question them, which is really quite absurd if you actually took the time to think about it."

Sadam heaved a heavy sigh. "This is now getting far too ridiculous. Are you saying that men like Moses, Muhammad and Jesus never existed?"

"I didn't say that," Alidore replied. "They did exist. Yet it was the fanatical nature of mankind that exalted 'good mortal men' to a status of 'supernatural divinity.' Jesus was a moral-minded man whose followers glorified him as the Son of God in the *Gospels*, while Moses fabricated much of this fantasy. For example, in *Genesis*, Moses stated that your God created man the day after all other creatures, which would also include dinosaurs. Yet because Moses knew nothing about dinosaurs, that blatant falsehood was written as God's Word. Worse yet, no devout Jew or Christian ever questioned it for thousands of years. Nor did they question why God so gloriously boasted about the Earth, while the heavens and stars were created just to give the night sky additional light. Hence, the endless expanse of trillions upon trillions of stars and planets throughout the universe, with countless other life forms, were of such insignificance as not to merit the slightest explanation. Yet Moses was just one of the flawed spinners of fiction, along with Zoroastrians, Buddhists, Hindus and your countless cults of antiquity. That yearning, or weakness, to create a god was one of many human traits that we Ultradorians found quite bizarre. Nothing like that has ever emerged on our planet, nor have we encountered that god-fabricating mentality with any other civilization we've encountered throughout the galaxy, which presently numbers over eighty thousand. Yet, the human species has this innate and desperate need to invent a higher being for security, out of fear or ignorance, in a vain attempt to make sense of this vast and complex universe. But even worse than those inept prophets are the trillions of foolish sheep who blindly believe them, as they're too lazy to even investigate their faith. For as I often say, *those who are unread are easily mislead.*"

Alidore paused briefly, making sure his inferior subjects had time to process these shocking facts, which he knew they would refuse to accept. Ultradorians had learned that once humans believed fervently in a religion or politics, they would rather fight and die than accept a conflicting truth that proved them wrong. Alidore also recalled the wise words of Mark Twain, who said, 'It's easier to fool people than to convince them that they've been fooled.'

He then continued, "We agree, that this is mindboggling in its breadth and complexity. However, we Ultradorians have always strived to find the answers ourselves, as logical scientists dedicated to seeking the truth, rather than prophets fabricating myths to pacify their ignorance. We were also amazed at how this trait of yours sprouted up at different locations on your planet, with diverse and bizarre gods being created in the eastern hemisphere as compared to the different and peculiar ones in the western hemisphere. None of which made the least bit of sense. The only common denominator among all your Earthly cults was the worship of the Light of the World, which was a saying you applied to Jesus, Allah, Apollo and even Augustus, among others. But in reality, it referred to your Sun. For the Sun does give this planet the opportunity to spring-forth biological life forms. And that's why we chose to do our experiment here. Earth is a very fertile planet. And that, my Earthly subjects, *is* the truth."

Sadam looked back up at the screen to see the infant boy, Adam, crawl out of the metallic atom, followed by the second capsule with a baby girl. He shook his head adamantly. "No! No! No way is this the truth! This is what Hollywood calls great CGI animation. And I'll gladly give you the Oscar for Special Effects." Angrily, he stood up and slammed his half-eaten sandwich down on the table. "You have insulted our intelligence long enough! I want out of here! Now!"

Alidore sighed. "And where exactly would you go, Sadam?"

Sadam's anger was smacked with cold reality, while his heart rate slowly simmered. He shook his head. *That* question was one Sadam truly couldn't answer. All he knew now was that he was in a nightmare with no escape. Mankind not only destroyed the once fertile and soothing world he knew, but it was now being twisted upside down by these ugly creatures claiming to be their makers. Dejectedly, he knew there was no place to go, and he stood mute as his shoulders slumped.

Meanwhile, Alidore continued, "The truth, once again, is that your species destroyed your entire planet. With a breakdown in governance, more than three-quarters of your entire population became useless, as crime and lethargy escalated to unprecedented levels. What we learned is that the vast majority of the human species is uneducated and rendered indolent by welfare programs that dish out money and food, but offer no skills of how to be self sufficient. And that's all under the ludicrous guise of being humane and compassionate. Every continent, except Antarctica, was plagued with this human-created disease. Yet most of you never learned to embrace the phrase you invented, and that is *tough love*. Tough love would have given those people the resources they needed most to carve out a productive life, like education, not things like free food, housing and health benefits and expecting nothing in return. Worse yet, these uneducated and unproductive bottom-feeders were given money, food, medicine and even luxuries, all paid for by your hardworking middle-class taxpayers under your failed experiment of socialism. And what did you do to the most productive of your species? The middle-class were burdened with great financial losses, as well as health issues, caused by the stress of living just to fund these suicidal programs."

"Yes, we've made mistakes," Evelyn finally retorted. "But our compassion served us extremely well, too. Loving one another, especially through the auspices of great religious charities, which you mock, has helped millions of people. And there's no denying that believing in God inspired Michelangelo and Leonardo to create artwork that represents the pinnacle of artistic endeavors, or how the sacred music by the great composers reached the most sublime level of music ever conceived. Just listen to Bach's *Mass in B Minor* or Liszt's *Christus Oratorio* to hear proof of what I say. None of that could have ever been obtained if they didn't fervently believe in the one and only true God, Jesus Christ."

"Yes, there was a good side to humanity," Alidore conceded. "However, those artists and composers achieved greatness due to inspiration for the particular project at hand. Just as they could obtain the same pinnacle of mastery for other secular endeavors, such as Michelangelo's sculptures of the Medicis or Leonardo's portraits, with his *Mona Lisa* being largely accepted as the greatest painting of all time. Those motivations were simply to be the best, both personally and or competitively. Similarly, the inspiration that made Michael Jordan the greatest basketball player was not due to his belief in God, but rather, as he said, his competitive drive to better himself and his intense obsession to prove the naysayers wrong. Mankind just needs a goal to believe in with full conviction to achieve success, be that in their own abilities or fueled by competition to attain the seemingly impossible. There is nothing religiously magical about it. It's just the best part of your human DNA."

As Evelyn and Sadam remained mute, assessing Alidore's disturbing yet meaningful words of logic, Alidore continued, "You humans also boasted of quite a few truly great individuals, such as Archimedes, Galileo, Newton, Curie, Pasture, Einstein, Fermi, Wozniak and others, but, as I said, very few over the course of countless centuries. We learned that of the ten billion people that inhabited your planet this year, only forty-three were brilliant enough to effect major changes. Not small stepping-stones, I'm talking about *huge milestones*. Events like the industrial revolution, the invention of electricity to power your world, aeronautical and aerospace technologies to give you flight, the invention of the computer to offer a myriad of spectacular endeavors, or the creation of the Internet to communicate globally. As you can see by your past history, it only had a handful of brilliant minds per era, such as those like Archimedes, Shakespeare, Tesla, Henry Ford or Von Braun. However, just a handful per era is a horrifically pitiful number by our standards."

Sadam smirked as he heatedly sat back down. "And what are your planet's godly statistics?"

Alidore looked his way. "As I said, the term god is not one in our lexicon. It's a fabrication of the human mind. But to answer your question, our planet consists of twelve billion, and more than half of those are of superior quality, the rest are of typical intellect and ability. Yet all contribute to our society. We have no failures. And that statistic does not focus on knowledge alone, like you humans so foolishly do, by boasting of college degrees and IQs, as if those things really determine what constitutes true brilliance."

Evelyn shook her head. "Well, I sure as hell would never allow a doctor to do brain surgery on me without a doctorate's degree."

Alidore smiled. "Yes, granted, there are some trades that require a degree for learning specialized skills that are necessary. Even we five have studied biology in our academy for four thousand years before entering into practice. However, look at some of those earthly names mentioned already, such as Archimedes, Da Vinci, Galileo, Newton, Edison, Ford and others, including college dropouts like Bill Gates or Steve Jobs. None of them had college degrees. Yet diplomas became the norm in your world, ignoring the obvious fact that *they* were the superstars of their eras, shinning brightly amid a dark, indolent mass of mediocrity."

Lasidore finally interjected, "Allow me to touch upon another topic, Sadam; one that I hope will enlighten you, yet I'm sure will likewise upset you."

Sadam heatedly turned his gaze his way. "And what's that?"

Lasidore looked at Sadam intently with his black, deep-set eyes. "This refers to you and your cult in particular. We also learned what became very apparent in the human species, yet many of you considered so taboo as to dare even mention. And that is the intelligence and innovative productivity of your different races and religions."

Sadam rolled his eyes and squirmed in his chair with heated anticipation, as Lasidore relayed the statistics: "The world population of Muslims had contributed very little in the way of engineering, technology, medicine and various trades when compared to others, focusing far more on religion and the many hours demanded of them for prayer and obedience to your god."

Once again, Sadam sprung to his feet! "Who are you, *allegedly brilliant*, people to analyze and criticize *us* humans, when you wasted millions of years observing us with no moral purpose to step in and save us from destroying this planet?"

Calidore chimed in, being the most abrasive of the lot, chiding, "We *invented* the human race! It was our brilliant biological formulations that gathered the atoms necessary to make you and every other life form on this planet. If you think that requires little to no intelligence, you are truly more primitive than we thought! Then again, that humans believed the Earth was the center of the universe for thousands of years, until Galileo proved the church wrong, only testifies how gullible and stupid most humans are. Nevertheless, our mission was a scientific one, not a charity case. Your sole purpose was for enlightening our superior minds with scientific data, not for us to coddle your primitive species with morals and a helping hand."

Alidore cut in, "Calidore, *please*, you know how we Ultradorians loath arrogance. Your temper too often unleashes your unruly tongue. *Enough!* We don't wish to insult or upset our guests. They have lived through a traumatic and cataclysmic event, being the only two to survive. Let's give them more time to process all these disturbing revelations."

"*Disturbing* is an understatement," Sadam gripped. He looked back at Lasidore. "So, tell me, now that you demeaned my entire Muslim brotherhood, what other racist revelations do you have?"

Lasidore pursed his lips. "We know this is hard to fathom, so perhaps Alidore is right. Maybe we should allow you both a few days to process all of this. After all, your minds are… well, let's just move onward. Perhaps you need rest?"

Evelyn and Sadam clenched their fists, as Sadam barked, "No! We don't need rest; sleepwalking into this nightmare is bad enough. But let's just continue the horror show, shall we?"

"As you wish," Lasidore said calmly. "As for the breakdown of races, it was abundantly and irrefutably made manifest that Europeans, who also migrated to the Western hemisphere, had contributed the most innovations and progress to the world than all other races combined. And they —"

"Hogwash!" Sadam interrupted, as he shook his head and angrily sat back down. "That *is* refutable. After all, the magnificent architecture of the Süleymaniye Mosque in Istanbul is a marvel of engineering. And we invented arithmetic in Mesopotamia, well before Western nations."

Lasidore offered a pedagogic smile, and said, "The Süleymaniye Mosque was merely a larger copy of the Hagia Sophia, which was built by the Romans almost a thousand years earlier. And yes, arithmetic was indeed advanced significantly by brilliant men like Al-Khwarizmi and Al-Battani, very noble achievements, yet its greatest uses were by the West many centuries later for engineering and technological marvels. So, I'm afraid your kin, including great men like Al-Jazari and Al-Razi, contributed far less than the West on the grand scale of innovative progress."

Sadam sneered, "That is simply beyond racist!"

"And why would we be racist?" Lasidore replied. "We are not even human. So what impetus would we have to play favorites? I assure you in all honesty, we have no agenda, and are unlike your politicians, who sold their souls to any other race or creed, no matter how hostile to their own kind, all for greed, power, or both. They are prime examples of hypocrites and traitors, who also exhibited very racist traits."

"Well, you got one thing right," Sadam barked. "You're certainly *not* human!" Sadam's lips twisted and his eyes rolled in thought. "But my mind keeps circling back to *why*, why would you invent us, as you said, and then watch us destroy ourselves? That's extremely hard to comprehend. You talk of being so brilliant and a higher order of species than us, and even dis our gods, yet you have no souls, no love, no compassion. So what good are *you*!"

Jasidore glanced at her comrades sheepishly, then at the humans, and admitted, "Well, the fact is, I did try to help you. Shackleton's ship did sink to the bottom of the Weddell Sea, right here in Antarctica. I raised the stern to help you at least weather the storm."

The Ultradorians all looked at her, appalled, as Alidore said, "Why would you do that?"

Jasidore looked back at Alidore. "Because we have worked so hard on this Earthly experiment for millions of years, Alidore. It was sad to see them ruin everything. I figured by letting them see the ship's name, *Endurance*, that that would inspire them to keep trying to rebuild their species and a better world." She looked back at Evelyn. "And, Shackleton and his crew *did* survive that expedition, Evelyn. With great endurance, they managed to use their lifeboats to return to safety. It was a miraculous feat of survival that I had hoped you two would find inspirational. Too bad you didn't know that part of your history."

Alidore shook his head, then looked at Sadam. "So, you see, we do have compassion, and sadly, it points out, once again, that humans rarely know or learn from their history."

He shook his head, disappointed at Jasidore's interference and the humans' ignorance, then continued, "But as we said numerous times, we are what you call scientists. We are objective observers of the biological experiments we created. To interfere would only negate the entire exercise, and render it useless. Our purpose is to study the habits of our specimens, and that can only be done by not interfering. Your scientists did the same thing."

Alidore rubbed his head, realizing this was going to be harder than he thought, as he continued, "Once again, it's a very odd human trait to fabricate a god, and to think that He, not She, which *is* quite sexist, actually knows and cares about each and everyone of you individually, and steps in when He hears your prayers for better health, a better job, or better this or better that, or good fortune. And all the while you irrationally pray to a contrived illusion that resides in a black and vast universe, which is inhumanly hostile and frigid, where no heavenly white clouds of Paradise exist. Except, of course, in your whimsical minds. Even Earth's location is nothing divinely unique or miraculous. Yet your scriptures foolishly glorify Earth as being the center of the universe and the only planet to which your God gave intelligent life. On the contrary, this tiny and insignificant speck, called Earth, resides on the distant outskirts of this galaxy, lost among trillions and trillions of other planets scattered across a seemingly endless universe. And many other species exist in that vast universe that are far more intelligent, innovative and admirable than this flawed human experiment we crafted."

Alidore sighed, genuinely disappointed at humankind's ludicrous obsession with mythmaking, which only crippled intellectual growth, as he took a deep breath, and continued, "You all spend a great deal of time praying for good things to happen and designate all marvelous events as being fulfilled by your God. Yet you rarely, if ever, contemplate the trillions upon trillions of unanswered prayers. Or worse yet, the heartless deaths of millions of innocent children dying of cancer in your hospitals, or the six million Jews brutally massacred in Hitler's holocaust, or the twenty million Russians, Slavs and Mongolians who were ruthlessly killed by Stalin, or the billions of tragedies that afflicted countless people over many centuries with horrible diseases, plagues or wars, all of which still baffles us. If you truly had a loving and all-powerful flawless God, how could he do such inhumane and destructive acts? What morals did *He* offer or instill in *you*?"

As Sadam and Evelyn sat speechless, Masidore now chimed in, "And yet you sit here and blame us for not intervening. Your illogical self-made and self-destructive belief systems fail to offer us the slightest bit of confidence in you having any serious degree of intelligence. And your self-inflicted genocide is the ultimate verdict of your shameful and destructive breed. You're no different than the gullible fools who worshiped Jim Jones in your zeal for false gods and to blindly commit your own suicide. Moreover, you polluted your land, seas, and air in industrial pursuits deemed as progress, tampered with nature by seeding clouds to alter climate, only to cause mounting hurricanes, tornadoes, wildfires and tsunamis that wreaked havoc all across the globe. And then your treasonous politicians opened borders, allowing unvetted illegal criminals in to rape and kill your citizens, while the unproductive lot littered your streets with homeless tents and feces that literally destroyed your once laudable civilization. America, Germany, England, France all exhibited these suicidal tendencies that defy any sense of logic, since *they* let the terrorists in to take over and destroy their own nations. It's truly appalling."

Calidore chimed in with his invectives. "We just can't comprehend the stupidity. After thousands of years of evolution, the human race learned very little from their mistakes. And by what we've learned, it was also due to your species not teaching new generations about the past, including their nation's laws, and the good and bad things that happened. Your most recent younger generations were sadly devoid of knowing anything about your laudable figures to emulate, nor did they learn about the villains who were destructive, thereby almost ensuring that they'd make the same mistakes. Not to mention the breakdown in family structure, where parents either coddled or ignored their children. So, my final verdict of the human race, despite its many good points, rests largely on one thing, their utter *stupidity!*"

Calidore paused briefly, seething, then continued his reprimand. "And let's not forget how your wanton self-centered madness even killed every other species on this planet, including Earth's natural resources to even offer life." Heatedly, he looked up at the screen, which now displayed various views of the catastrophic apocalypse, then back at the humans, and added, "And *that* horrifying wasteland outside validates the only thing human's truly create... *Destruction!*"

Sadam and Evelyn had sat smoldering during the Ultradorians' lengthy lectures, or in Calidore's case, castigations, for far too long. They wanted to get up and leave, but as Alidore had rightfully stated, where would they go? They were not only drifters without a home; they were drifters without a human race. Moreover, their race had indeed destroyed the entire planet out of sheer stupidity, a fact that they hated to admit but knew in their hearts. And as they stared at the ugly creatures before them, they couldn't believe that they were at the top of the food chain, or worse yet, that they had created humans, animals and plants in a global Petri dish just to be studied like bacteria.

Meanwhile, Alidore's head had lowered in thought and sympathy. Then he looked up at each of them, and said, "Well, I do apologize for us having to inject harsh truth and reality into your disillusioned minds, but there it is." He peered at his four fellow scientists then back at the humans. "Unfortunately, our experiment has finally ended. We anticipated a much brighter outcome, but as I said, that was entirely left up to your species. With this disastrous state we now find ourselves in, it is time for us to depart and return home to our planet. Ultradore is at the far side of this galaxy, some ninety-four light-years away, and is a journey your kind had often dreamt about yet never attained the knowhow to achieve. I must be honest; Ultradore's orbit is the farthest from the small sun in our solar system. As such, it is extremely frigid, hence, why we chose this location in your south pole to setup our headquarters."

A chilling revelation now occurred to Sadam and Evelyn, far more chilling than the Ultradorian planet. Namely, if the Ultradorians were leaving, what happens to them?

Alidore then finally delivered that ultimatum. "Therefore, as we never interfered or governed your actions, we now ask you for your preference; will you stay here or come with us?"

Sadam and Evelyn's minds went blank with foreboding as the reality of their very existence, and possibly the future existence of a new generation of humankind rested solely upon their decisions.

Calidore, impatient and arrogant as ever, pressed, "*Well!* What will it be, humans?"

Alidore waved his hand, cautioning Calidore to stop, as his large black eyes veered back at the dazed humans. "Sadam, Evelyn, I know this is a monumental decision, yet the nature of serendipity does have a strange appearance here. For your very names, if we subtract the *S* from Sadam and delete the *lyn* of Evelyn leaves you with Adam and Eve. Perhaps it was meant for you to start again."

Sadam and Evelyn seemed to be awakened by that revelation, never piecing it together, but now looked at each other in a new light. They truly felt blessed and chosen for this critical task. As smiles of love and a bright future illuminated their once forlorn faces, Calidore ruined the moment. "Now don't let your silly beliefs make you think that that was by divine providence or granted by some vaporous god of yours! Remember, there are no gods, just us Ultradorians."

As Sadam and Evelyn both frowned, Alidore interjected, "Calidore, temper your remarks, please! These humans don't need to hear your reprimands."

"Yes, they do!" Calidore retorted. "If they intend to re-jumpstart their species, they must begin with a clear mindset and learn from their mistakes." Calidore's face twisted with animus. "And the audacity of the human species to think that their fake god made man in *His* image! As if humans, on this tiny dot of a planet, lost in an endless universe, was that special. What would that make *us*, Alidore? We certainly were not made in His or their image, and yet we are far superior, as are thousands of other species we know of across this galaxy, each very different looking than the next. Yet by their foolish religion, we all would be *heretics*! Their ridiculous and intolerant self-importance is as mindboggling as it is maddening. And how they could believe that an all-knowing and allegedly *perfect* god would send his son down to Earth to *enlighten the world*, yet only in the tiny town of

Nazareth to preach to the most illiterate and uneducated lot in Judea, and have a ministry that only lasted one year, is beyond imperfect, it's ludicrous. So, let me say this, we are what they would call their gods, if such a fantasy existed. So, as their godly creators, shouldn't we decide what our experiment's futures should be?"

Alidore sighed. "Calidore, you are well aware that our project was setup by us, but was one we would never interfere with. The decisions are theirs to make. As an intelligent Utradorian, don't let me have to repeat that again." Alidore turned and looked back at Sadam and Evelyn. "So, have you reached a decision?"

Evelyn looked at Sadam, who gazed back into her sapphire eyes. The radiant glow had gone, as the solemn look on her face eerily mirrored his own. With their hearts and hopes blackened by the nightmare of starting over on a toxic planet radiated and doomed, they knew it was hopeless. And to live on a distant frigid planet with aliens who would treat them as inferior experiments or pets was also a gruesome dead end for them and the human race.

They turned and looked at Alidore, as each swiftly grabbed a knife off the table and impaled each other. As their limp bodies fell to the floor, Alidore and his cadre were flabbergasted, except for Calidore, who sniggered. "I knew these pathetic creatures would make the wrong decision."

Alidore irritably glared at Calidore, then gazed down at the dead bodies. A tear trickled down from his eye. Overwhelmed with sympathy, he uttered, "I find it extremely sad. They never even asked us if we could eradicate all the toxins of planet Earth."

Calidore sniggered. "Yes, like I said… *Stupid!*"

CONQUESTS, COUPS & COLLAPSE

In the rolling seas of the Caribbean, Sir Walter Raleigh was at the helm heading back home to England. King James I was impatiently awaiting his arrival to answer for his violation of Spanish laws when his men attacked a Spanish outpost in South America. Not only was Sir Walter responsible for his men's actions, but of equal importance, Raleigh had breached the terms of his pardon from prison just a year ago for treason.

It was October 13, 1618, and last year Raleigh had been released and commissioned by King James to search for the enticing legend of El Dorado; its mission, to clutch a hefty windfall of gold to fill the king's coffers. However, this was Raleigh's second attempt at finding the elusive jackpot and, once again, his mission found nothing but hot tropical rainforests infested with mosquitoes.

Despite the charges against him, Raleigh was only too eager to leave the smothering humidity of South America, as he yelled out to his first mate, "Hoist the sails, Henry. We're setting a course north, along the coast to thirty degrees latitude. From there, crossing the Atlantic will take us closer to home.

"Aye, aye, Captain!" Henry replied.

Raleigh turned toward his navigator. "William, that should take us about two leagues past Bermuda, then we'll head due east."

William complied, and the ship cut through the choppy waves bearing north. As they sailed, Sir Walter's mind drifted back to his eleven years in prison. Having been incarcerated in the Tower of London on false charges of treason, he had decided to make good use of his idle time. He penned over 1100 pages of his tome *History of the World,* yet never finished the larger outline he had envisioned.

Despite being a bold adventurer and one of Queen Elizabeth's favorite courtiers, he had a fervid interest in history. The hallowed names of courageous leaders, like Alexander and Caesar, who conquered foreign lands, intrigued him, as well as the machinations of politics that proved equally exciting and lethal. The thrill was the fuel that sparked his vibrant spirit, and being a prominent Englishman, staking claims in the New World for Elizabeth, and now for James, he took a deep breath, confident that his pleas to the king will dissolve this frivolous complaint by the Spanish crown.

Raleigh's daydream was broken when Henry called out, "Captain, Bermuda is just up ahead, but there is an alarming tempest heading our way!"

Sir Walter turned and gasped. The ominous black hurricane was massive! It seemed to come out of nowhere and was nothing like anything he had ever seen. He bellowed, "Lower the sails, without delay!"

Hurriedly he looked for his navigator, but William stood paralyzed in shock at the wheel. Raleigh rushed over and nudged William aside as he grabbed the wheel and cut the rudder hard right. But it was too late; lightning shattered the dark sky as webs of electricity zapped the waves all around them. One bolt struck the mast, vaporizing its iron cap.

Crewmen dashed to and fro readying the ship, but that, too, was in vain, as the ship listed and turned as the violent sea's waves splashed across the deck. The sky grew menacingly black, as visibility was cut down to a mere few feet. Raleigh ordered the crew below deck, save for six men to weather the storm. The minutes felt like hours as the ship was battered and the blustering winds pelted the seamen's faces. That their beloved ship was named *Destiny* now seemed like a bad joke.

With the tempest slightly starting to break up, Raleigh steered the ship through the dense black clouds, until Henry called out, "Land ho! I see a lighthouse, Captain."

Raleigh wiped the burning seawater out of his eyes to see a startling sight! There, before them, stood a colossal statue of the Emperor Claudius. Easily five times the height of their ship's tallest mast, Raleigh and the crew looked up in awe. To the left, the lighthouse looked tiny in comparison, yet it was a sight to behold, as the crew from below came up onboard and also praised the flashing light. The safety of land was now within reach.

As the ship sailed into the large harbor, the ominous black and twisted clouds parted as a beam of sunlight shone through the hellish sky.

The crew all jumped and cheered for their safe return to land, yet Sir Walter stood mute, his face grave, for he knew something was wrong, *very* wrong.

As Henry and William approached him with grins, they both stopped dead in their tracks, as Henry asked, "Captain, what's the matter? We made it through the hellish gale."

Raleigh broke his dead stare and looked at his first mate. "Henry, I know of no port that has a colossal statue of Claudius. Do you?"

As Henry squinted, just now giving that some thought, Sir Walter gazed at William. "Do you?"

William's lips twisted, perplexed. "Uh, no, Captain. But I assume it must be some new settlement by the Spaniards or Portuguese. After all, the North American continent is largely open to conquest. So that's the only logical answer."

Raleigh sighed. "Somehow it doesn't seem like logic applies here, William. Why would the Spaniards or Portuguese build a gargantuan statue to the Roman Emperor Claudius? It doesn't make sense. Not one bit."

William's face filled with doubt as trepidation seeped into his bones. He turned and looked at the shoreline. "Well, I can see people in the distance. So, we'll know soon enough."

Henry rubbed his wiry beard, now also nervous but cautious. "Captain, should I have the men ready their firearms?"

Sir Walter nodded. "Yes, but keep them out of sight. We don't want to appear as the aggressors. But if they start, we *shall* finish."

With that, the crew readied themselves for the unknown. As they approached the dock, the crew's eyes widened, some with bewilderment and others with amusement. Standing on the dock was a group of men, some dressed in Roman tunics, while the soldiers wore *galea* helmets and *lorica segmentatas*.

Henry glanced at William. "This must be a masquerade or some odd ritual by the Spaniards. After all, their matadors dress up and do wild things, too."

As William and others laughed, Raleigh raised his hand and commanded, "Silence!"

As they all cowered and gazed his way, he continued, "This does *not* look like a costume party or a bull fight." He glanced back at the colossal statue of Claudius, then back at the Romans on the dock. Being an avid reader and historian himself, Sir Walter knew something ungodly had just befallen him and his crew. With foreboding, he said, "Men, I want you all to stay onboard, and keep your firearms ready. I am going ashore alone, and unarmed. If anything happens to me, Henry, you set sail straight away. Is that understood?"

Henry echoed the thoughts of all, as he pleaded, "Captain, there is no way we would ever leave if you're in harm's way. If these men try anything stupid, we *will* attack in full measure."

Raleigh shook his head adamantly. "No! I'm already in trouble with King James for violating our peace agreements with Spain and have to stand trial, so I don't wish to aggravate the situation further. Only if I give the signal should you commence an attack. Is that understood?"

Dejectedly, Henry and the crew nodded in agreement.

With that, Sir Walter Raleigh disembarked and walked cautiously toward the Romans.

A dignified elderly Roman, wearing a tunic and sandals, stepped forward to greet him. The man looked at Raleigh's elaborate clothing with bewilderment. Sir Walter was well known for his flamboyant attire, as he wore a purple doublet with pearl buttons, gray breeches with white silk stockings, and fine leather shoes with a large silver buckle. The Roman smiled, amused, as he said in Latin, *"Salve!"*

Raleigh, being fluent in Latin, responded, *"Grates tibi."*

In Latin, the Roman said, "My name is Marcus. By your accent, I assume you are from Britannia, yes?"

"Indeed I am," Raleigh replied, well aware of the name by which the Roman's had labeled his homeland. Yet his mind was still trying to make sense of this surreal encounter, and he had to start probing, as he said, "My name is Walter." He looked around and added, "Where are we and what day is this?"

Marcus' reply truly struck Raleigh like a lightning bolt to the head, illuminating his hunch, for it was indeed the Port of Claudius in Ostia, October 13, 54 AD!

Raleigh gasped and shook his head in disbelief. He felt nauseous. How can this be!? his mind screamed. The tempest had only lasted twenty minutes, so it was impossible to have been windblown across the entire breadth of the Atlantic, he thought. Not to mention being blown back centuries in time to ancient Rome.

He looked at Marcus, then back up at the colossal statue of Claudius. Unnervingly, it all made sense. Having read *The Twelve Caesars* by Suetonius, he knew that Claudius had built the huge port, and seeing the colossal statue of him drove home the chilling reality.

A Roman soldier walked over with his hand on the hilt of his gladius. "I overheard you say you're from Britannia."

Seeing the soldier's aggressive stance, Raleigh snapped out of his stupor and replied, "Yes, I am! I sail for the king of—" he stopped short, realizing his error.

The soldier stepped closer. "What king!?" he barked, as he drew out his gladius and pointed the tip at Raleigh's face. "Aulus Plautius puts down any kings he encounters there, so which king is this you speak of?"

"My mistake," Raleigh said as he raised both hands in compliance. "Actually, we left because we no longer wish to serve him. May he fall to Plautius like the rest."

"Indeed he will!" the soldier growled.

Marcus interjected, "Walter, I strongly suggest that you set sail, as I unfortunately received disturbing news just an hour ago. Emperor Claudius has mysteriously been murdered in a coup, which many suspect was by his wife Agrippina so she could place her son Nero on the throne."

The soldier added sardonically, "Yes, and Rome is no place for barbarians, even if they are feline in nature, wearing colorful dainty clothing."

Raleigh's manly pride and loyalty to his king had been insulted once too many times, and throwing caution to the wind, he replied, "I shall indeed cast off, as this is more unnatural of a place than you think. But know this," he said turning his gaze at the soldier, "You Romans may boast of conquering Britannia and other places now, but Rome *will* collapse and fall, and England *will* become the world leader!"

The soldier squinted, not knowing what England meant, yet he was annoyed enough to not listen further. He swung his gladius in a threatening circular motion, and barked, "You are obviously drunk or stupid, barbarian. So best you take the advice of Marcus, our level-headed tribune, and sail your hides out of here before I turn you all into carrion to feed the rats!"

Sir Walter snarled. Not having his sword to defend his honor, he bid Marcus farewell and retorted to the blustering soldier, "Enjoy your fleeting time now, soldier, because your lives *will* become hell under Nero."

With that, Raleigh returned to the ship.

Setting a course for England, the crew was eager to get back home, but was still frightened and baffled. The startling reality of having sailed into the past was just too hard to fathom. *How will we ever get back to our own time and loved ones?* many asked with dread. As the cacophony of fear and bewilderment escalated, two sailors fainted and five vomited.

The panic and confusion only ceased once their attention was diverted by a strange yet familiar observation. Remnants of that peculiar storm, which had ushered them through time, still lingered in the Mediterranean Sea, and they were headed right back into the thick of it!

With all hands on deck, the *Destiny* was once again battered with rain and wind as it passed the Straits of Gibraltar and was blown out into the Atlantic.

This time they managed to steer *Destiny* toward the destiny *they* sought, and with luck they saw the port of Plymouth. Riding the less turbulent outer rim of the storm, they sailed into the harbor. The crew cheered and some even cried with relief, having landed back in England. Eager to forsake their ill-fated *Destiny*, thirteen crewmembers hopped over the side, only too glad to rush back home.

As Henry lowered the gangplank, Sir Walter walked down and called out, "I hope your fleeing my ship does not indicate cowardice and abandonment, oh, brave men of England, honoring King James the First?"

The crew stopped in their tracks and looked back at their captain, feeling half ashamed and half desperate to get back home to their families. They looked at one another, then obediently walked back toward their captain, as a series of pleas rang out: "I'm sorry," "Forgive me, Captain," "Our honor lies with you and the king, Captain," and the like.

Yet as the remaining crew disembarked the ship, Raleigh was overcome with an unsettling feeling. As he scanned the area, there were no buildings he had recalled seeing from his last visit, nor was there anyone in sight. The once bustling port was rustic and quiet, with only a small cabin. He turned toward his crew. "Men, stay put. I shall return."

With that, Raleigh walked over to the cabin and, as he entered, his poor eyes bulged, once again! Sitting at a desk was a young clerk dressed in a tunic, scribbling notes on a piece of papyrus.

The man rose to his feet and said in Latin, "Welcome, stranger. Where are you from and what is your business?"

Walter nearly collapsed and had to steady himself. Rubbing his forehead, he mumbled with a stutter, "Sir W- Walter Raleigh."

The Roman clerk stepped out from behind his desk and walked closer. "I didn't quite catch that?" he said in Latin.

"Sir Walter Raleigh!" he exclaimed, this time awakened from his time-altering trance. "And I am from England, yes, *England!* This very land you have invaded, the land of King James the First!"

The Roman was perplexed by Raleigh's agitated outburst, and replied, "Calm down, Sir Raleigh. You obviously are disturbed and confused. Perhaps too much time at sea has made you delirious. I've seen this affliction before."

Raleigh gritted his teeth, then blasted, "I am *not* delirious!" He looked around, still not believing the nightmare of which he had been cursed with. "This *crazy world* is delirious!"

Just then the sound of hooves trampling dirt diverted his attention as he looked back out the window. A group of twenty Roman soldiers on horseback came galloping up to the cabin. Coming to a brisk stop, the leader hopped off and walked toward Raleigh, who had already exited the cabin.

Walking with a commanding gait, the leader was wearing his full regalia: a decorative *galea* helmet, a bronze *lorica musculata* breastplate with bas-reliefs of Vespasian, Titus and Mars, and a long flowing purple *paludamentum* that flapped in his wake.

Coming face to face, he scanned Raleigh's flamboyant attire, then said, "I am Gnaeus Agricola, governor and pontificate of Britannia. As you can see, word travels fast in my province." He glanced at the huge ship, then back at

Raleigh. "Who are you, and what's the name of your tribe? I've never seen a vessel like yours, nor such flashy clothes."

Although Raleigh was distraught at being marooned in an ancient time zone he was enthralled to actually meet Agricola in person. He had read much about Agricola's early years in Britain, winning victory after victory, even riding with Paulinus to defeat Boudicca, the warrior queen, but that was as a *legate*. That Agricola said he was governor and pontificate, Raleigh knew this was toward the end of his stay in Britain.

Raleigh didn't wish to relay his time-traveling misadventure, as it would never resonate and only cause unnecessary confusion and possible conflict, as he replied, "I am Sir Walter Raleigh, and my tribe is one that resides very far from here. In fact, so far, that even we might have trouble returning, as we were blown off course."

Agricola eyed up the stranger. "I take it you are seeking to lay claim to a territory for your own tribe, then, yes?"

Raleigh was still unsure how to play this game, but being up against one of Rome's most successful military leaders, he opted for caution, and said, "No, Governor, not conquest, just a place to rest for a few days. As you can see, we are very experienced seafarers, and we must try to find our way back home."

Raleigh couldn't stop thinking about this miraculous encounter with a man who played a significant role in his nation's history, but his mind kept jumping back to all the Celts, Druids and Britons he had slain to conquer this territory, a province that he knew the Romans would abandon in roughly three hundred and twenty-five years from this very moment.

What was it all for? His mind growled. Raleigh's anger suddenly tempered with sympathy for his kin, as conquest was a double-edged sword. And being at the opposite end of victory made Raleigh's lips twist with annoyance, as he said, "Actually, your many victories here have also traveled very far and fast. As a *legate* you killed thousands of Britons." He looked around, and added, "And for what? What changed, other than you being able to rule over these people who fought tooth and nail to oppose you?"

Agricola's demeanor turned from conqueror to creator, as he replied, "There will always be the whiners and the winners, Sir Raleigh. If you knew anything about conquest you'd know as I have learned that we cannot please everyone. But you ask, what changed? I say, an extraordinary number of things have changed. I found this island inhabited by primitive tribes that lived only marginally better than the animals they slaughtered for food. They lived in mud or leather huts, cooked on open pits, never knew what warm mineral baths were, had no idea how to manipulate water with aqueducts, they had no stone roads to enhance ease of travel and communication, no mills to mass produce grain, no sturdy, stone architectural edifices to last for centuries, no code of laws to maintain order and efficiently manage civil disputes, no organized educational programs to ensure progress, for I instilled Latin into all the youths of nobles, so these people will one day have a common language, rather than the mayhem and wars they had among themselves."

Agricola huffed. "I hear the same gripes from many Britons, *Why must you rule over us?* Yet, such gripes are borne out of either fear of losing their primitive heritage or ignorance of not recognizing progress, as raising barbarians up to become civilized is a noble enterprise, one not easy to execute or maintain. Yet it was brave and wise men like Emperors Vespasian and Titus who instructed men like me and others to make it so."

Raleigh's seething bitterness subsided into a silence of profound scrutiny. He had studied the exploits of great military men and their bloody deeds, deeds of adventure he enjoyed himself. Yet that Queen Elizabeth had entrusted him to colonize the New World, by simply claiming land for personal gain, or how King James now commissioned him to seek gold in South America, just to strip and rape the resources of lands inhabited by others, now struck him as being just as primitive as his ancient Celt and Druid ancestors living in mud huts and killing each other.

He looked at Agricola with new eyes, realizing the system of Romanization was superior to England's colonization. Where his king and queen just sought riches for their own needs, the Romans sought unity by sharing their successful culture and progress. Of course he also knew the ugly side of slavery and harsh punishments that afflicted all peoples of ancient times, but Raleigh looked upon the world and his own life differently now and had hopes of changing his actions for a brighter future.

He now envisioned a new course that he felt compelled to explain to King James, in essence, to plead for a reprieve for the attacks on Spanish soil and presenting a new industrious and uplifting method for their New World ventures by enhancing the lives of natives while uniting the world in cultural harmony. He now realized that the primitive natives who refused to accept advancements where just pigheaded, and that the mission to uplift and educate these people would never be easy, but it was a noble effort worth the struggle.

Converted and committed to his new philosophy, Sir Walter said, "I stand corrected, Governor Agricola. You have done an honorable job and have enlightened me, as well." He now recognized that many of the advances England enjoyed were based on Roman introductions to their archaic island. And the fact that even the English language was largely based upon Latin roots, Raleigh realized the tremendous impact Rome had on their very heritage and culture.

Rubbing his forehead, Raleigh's mind veered back to the present, and that present had a different timeframe than his own present of 1618, a present now lost to time. Yet, having had the time to assess what Agricola said, Raleigh estimated the current date to be around 84 AD, as he added, "My only regret is having to tell you that your time here as governor is about to end."

"Yes, I'm sure of that," Agricola said. "I've played this role for seven years, far beyond any governor in our empire. If I last another year it will be a miracle."

"No, I'm afraid it will be a lot sooner than that," Raleigh said.

As Agricola squinted, baffled by Raleigh's remark, a messenger rode in fast on horseback and stopped short. As a dust cloud arose from his horse's hooves, he hopped off. Scurrying over to Agricola, he handed him a scroll with the Imperial wax seal.

Agricola grasped it, broke the seal, and began to read. As his eyes oscillated to the lines, his mind darted back to Raleigh's prediction, as he looked up and said, "How in blazes could you have known? Emperor Domitian is calling me back to Rome!"

Even Raleigh was shocked, as he stammered, "Well, I only f-figured your time as governor had to end soon. But not this soon."

Agricola shook his head. "Well, that was a mighty eerie prediction, Sir Walter. Perhaps you should accompany me back to Rome and place some wagers at the Circus Maximus. I would surely follow your lead."

Raleigh chuckled. "No, I'm sure my skills wouldn't be of any use on chariot races. But I will tell you that you need not worry about your political future, or the deadly game of politics any longer. I wish you a happy retirement, one you most certainly deserve."

Agricola still gazed at Raleigh as some sort of eccentric oracle. And the fact that he wore outlandish clothes and sailed on a strange vessel, the likes of which no one had ever seen before, seemed to all fit.

Meanwhile, Raleigh's crew had been getting anxious and now Raleigh himself was eager to leave. They had to try to get back home somehow, as he shook Agricola's forearm, in Roman fashion, and said, "We must ship off to find our way back home. It was an honor to meet you, Governor Agricola, and I bid you farewell!"

"Safe travels, Sir Walter Raleigh," Agricola responded.

Raleigh and his crew boarded *Destiny* and waved goodbye as they shoved off. As soon as the ship caught a healthy breeze and the sails and rigs were set, the weary crew circled around Raleigh.

Henry queried, "Captain, where to now?"

While William added, "Yes, what is our course, Captain?"

The nervous crew all mumbled similar refrains, when Raleigh said, "Simmer down, men. You all know I have as much knowledge about this nebulous tempest as you do. But one thing I do know. We caught that mysterious anomaly near Bermuda." He looked at William. "So set our course for that bewitched island."

The crew moaned with a shiver, as one called out, "But God knows where that cursed storm will blow us next, Captain?"

"Yeah, even our beloved England is no more!" another whined. "We're damned!"

"Calm down!" Raleigh ordered. "I will not have a crew of spineless eels, if that is what you've become, jump overboard this very second! Otherwise, *man* this ship and buckle up for the ride."

Like scolded children, the crew dispersed and quietly manned their stations.

As they sailed for days across the Atlantic, Raleigh had cleared his head and felt a renewed sense of confidence. He was sure that his new Romanized outlook would absolve the charges against him when he lands back home and… his mind hit a brick wall! Or rather, the wall of that dreadful tempest that would whisk them away to some other time and place. He shook his head, fretting what will happen even if they find this bewitched storm. As his crew feared, *where would they end up?*

The days turned into weeks as they sailed across a turbulent ocean. The clear skies, normally praised, were now viewed as bad omens. Even attempting to catch fish was proving to be a useless chore, as many lost their appetites and were numb with melancholy. They knew that they were marooned in an ancient world in which they didn't belong.

Sir Walter tried his best to uplift their sullied spirits, but the long and lonely weeks had taken their toll. Finally, Henry bellowed! "Land ho! Bermuda is on the horizon."

The lethargic crew managed to shuffle over to the port side and gazed at the darkening sky. Slowly, one by one, their spirits rose along with their adrenaline as the ominous tempest grew rapidly in size and venom. Within minutes, *Destiny* was blasted with sleet and wind as she listed almost to the point of capsizing. The crew panicked and dashed down below, while Raleigh, Henry and William attempted to maintain some control. Lightning briefly illuminated the menacing clouds, appearing like cannon fire and fireworks, both deafening and blinding.

Out of the corner of William's eye he saw something. Then as he looked head-on, he bellowed, "Glory be! That looks like England!"

Henry swiftly slid his way over the wet deck to William's side. He gazed out and exclaimed, "Land ho! Eng-LAND it is!"

As the tempest wound its way down and pushed them towards shore, the crew emerged from below and rushed to the railings.

"Glory be to God and the Highest! England it is!" one mate bellowed.

As another cheered. "Thank God, we're home. Finally home!"

"Hold on!" Raleigh yelled. "England it is, but we don't know what time we've sailed into. Temper your expectations until we get ashore."

With that, the crew took heed of the Captain's words and they manned their positions. As *Destiny* pulled into port, their hearts lifted. One sailor noticed all the buildings and familiar signage, and another even saw his friend walking along the pier. They knew the good Lord returned them home.

The crew broke out with euphoric cheers of godly praise as they tied the ropes to the deck cleats and fled like angels fleeing the fires of Hell. As some ran to meet friends or relatives, others literally kissed the ground and then looked up to heaven. And what a heavenly sight they saw, as an ethereal beam of sunlight vaporized the dark clouds, while the golden radiance of the sun warmed their very souls.

As Sir Walter strode down the gangplank, Henry bellowed, "Let's rally for Raleigh, our Earthly savior!"

The crew all turned and cheered, "Hail Sir Walter Raleigh!" with repetitious abandon.

Raleigh smiled, but responded humbly. "I had little hand in this miraculous journey, and glorious return. It's splendid to be home. But let us give thanks to the good Lord above!"

As the crew echoed his words, two constables approached Raleigh, as one barked, "Sir Walter Raleigh, you are under arrest!" While the other added, "By order of King James the First."

As the crew hissed and moaned, Raleigh waved for silence. "Men, we all knew I had to answer for the attacks made on the Spanish outpost, of which I take full reasonability, as that broke the agreement of my pardon. However, fear not. The new policies of which I shall present to the king will absolve me of all those infractions and establish a new era of meaningful exploration. Greater days lie ahead."

Only partially satisfied, the crew still mumbled under their breaths and shook their heads. Meanwhile, the two constables escorted Raleigh away and shoved him into a prison wagon.

Brought to the Tower of London, Raleigh was pushed into a cell. He rolled his eyes, seeing, once again, the dreadful cell that locked him up like an animal for eleven depressing years. Looking at the oppressive stonewalls; he had all to do to snap out of the doldrums that threatened to crush his spirits. The false charges that had landed him in this godforsaken dungeon dredged up all the bile in his gut of how justice is a fallacy, rarely served. With a grunt, he now questioned how God could do this to him, a patriot.

But then he shook his head: *Stop it!* his mind screamed. *You must stay positive. Once the king hears my pleas and benevolent new plans, this nightmare* will *end.*

It was October 27, 1618, and two days later, Sir Walter Raleigh was thunderstruck, as were many in the courtroom, when he was convicted of treason from his earlier trial (with pressure by the Spanish crown for the outpost attack), thus forcing the fatal hand of doom by King James.

However, the executioner, who stood above a kneeling Raleigh (whose head was on a block), would deliver the actual hand of doom.

Raleigh's head turned as he looked up and asked, "Let me see the axe, good man."

The executioner was startled by the request. Yet loathing his orders to execute a man he admired, he had no words, and simply extended his arm down, passing the blade before Raleigh's eyes, eyes destined to see the light of day for only a few more seconds.

Raleigh looked up at the solemn man dressed in black, and could see the regret in his face, as he quipped, "This is a sharp medicine, but it's a physician for all diseases and miseries. Don't burden your heart, for this deed is not of your doing, but that of a corrupt world and, what can only be deemed, a morbid or false god. Proceed."

He laid his head on the chopping block and kept his eyes open, reassessing his last visions of an ironic and cruel world, one he now believed strived to create godly wonders, yet inevitably succumbed to human blunders.

As Raleigh lamented these depressing thoughts he soon realized that he was still cognizant and his head was still attached to his body.

He glanced up at the vacillating executioner, and commanded, "What do you fear? Strike, man, *strike!*"

With a swift blow, the axe came down and Sir Walter Raleigh's head departed, hitting the ground with a thud, as his limp body keeled over.

The dynamic essence and worldly presence of the charismatic adventurer, Sir Walter Raleigh, was transformed into two cold heaps of flesh and bones, drenched in pools of blood. For the glorious and ghastly ways of the world stridently churn, as the hands of the clock forever turn.

EPILOGUE

Raleigh's wife, Elizabeth, was given his head, which she had embalmed, and kept it until the day she died. Rumors say it was then buried with their son Carew Raleigh.

As for Raleigh's beliefs in England's destiny to be the world's next superpower, that, too, was destined to follow that of Rome's, for it, too, would experience the Three C's, which all empires face: First Conquests, then Coups, then Collapse.

THE UNTOLD STORY OF ST. GEORGE

In the Roman province of Nicomedia, on February 22, 303 AD, a young and valiant Roman praetorian guard, named George, rode his winged, white stallion with the horn of a unicorn to Emperor Diocletian's villa.

Having been summoned to the palace, George was enamored how Diocletian proved to be a virtuous anomaly in the long line of Roman emperors. Ten years previously, Diocletian had done what no other ruler had done and decided to share his power with three others, thus forming a Tetrarchy. Having divided the sprawling empire into quarters, the four rulers had dominion over their select territory, yet consulted in unity. Diocletian's magnanimous decree was so astounding that it won the respect of not only George, but of the empire's entire citizenry, as well.

Before Diocletian's rise to power, however, the empire had suffered fifty years of mayhem, known as the Crisis of the Third Century. During those years the empire almost collapsed, as foreign invasions and internal fractures ignited civil wars, thus giving rise to a string of emperors and bloody coups. Yet with laudable skill, Diocletian ended the chaos and divided the empire into quadrants in an effort to be ruled more efficiently.

As George dismounted his strange and magnificent horse, Diocletian approached with wonder in his eyes. "What a beautiful animal you have, George. I was told many tales of its bizarre appearance, but to see it with my own eyes is truly a sight to behold."

George bowed and leaned his shield against a stone partition. "Thank you, Imperator Diocletian. Yes, Ascalon is indeed a one of kind miracle." George peered at his winged steed with affection and rubbed its long spindly horn. "And he has accompanied me in many battles, being even more valued than my sword for his impressive skills in combat."

"Yes, your lauded battle of slaying a dragon has garnered mythical proportions among the Christian sect, so I hear," Diocletian said, not truly knowing the full tale. "Where exactly did that take place?"

"It was in the town of Silene, which is in the province of Libya," George said.

He relayed how the dragon of great size and malice terrorized the town, to which the villagers offered two sheep each day as sacrifices to appease the wild beast. But having run out of livestock, the dragon now expected human sacrifices. The terrified villagers complied and chose someone each day to fulfill this gruesome demand. But when the villagers elected the proconsul's daughter to be offered as a sacrifice...

"That is when I rode into town and put an end to the evil madness," George said. "It was a brutal struggle, but my sword came down hard and fast and sliced the dragon to bits!"

Diocletian looked at George with admiration, yet his smile withered with concern. "But tell me, George. The rumors claim that the villagers converted to Christianity upon seeing this miraculous deed. Is that so?"

George's face wrinkled with concern. He knew that Diocletian's fellow emperor, Galerius, loathed Christians and engaged in bloody persecutions, but he wasn't sure of Diocletian's personal stance on the issue, as he uttered, "Yes, that is indeed true, Imperator. Does that offend you?"

Diocletian shrugged and shook his head tepidly. "No, no, not really. I harbor no animus against any cult in my empire, George. Yet, I'm sure you must have heard that Galerius and I have had heated arguments about these troublesome Christians?"

George nodded solemnly. "Yes, and it is most distressing. We Romans have always been very tolerant of other cults, even adopting aspects of their beliefs into our own pantheon of gods."

Diocletian twitched and rubbed his chin. He was unclear by George's remark, which displayed sympathy for the Christians yet ended with Roman pride of tradition. "So, George, what do *you* hold close to your heart, Roman beliefs or Christian dogma?"

"I must confess, Imperator, I am a devout Christian."

Diocletian looked deep into George's eyes. "Since I have yet to make a final judgment about this cult, I would like you to fulfill a task."

"Anything!" George exclaimed, eager to prove not only his worth but even more so, that of his cherished religion.

"There is a demon, so called by your fellow Christians, who is terrorizing Nicomedia. As you know, this is home to my palace, so no violence will I ever permit to ravish this land. And this demon has killed many Romans and Christians. What's more, he rides on a crimson horse with horns and the wings of a bat. From the terrifying stories I hear from the Christian community, they call this demon warrior Satan."

George flinched with fear, knowing that no mortal was a match for the Fallen Angel. "But, Imperator, Satan is not one to be slain so easily or at all, for he is the Master of All Evil and rides briefly among us in different forms. Moreover, he resides mostly in Hell, which you know as Hades."

"*Nothing* is impossible if one puts their mind to it, George!" Diocletian scolded. "And killing this Satan warrior is the task I need fulfilled. So, if you can accomplish this task, it will not only pacify Galerius and his hatred, but I will honor and defend Christianity with the full gravity of my bearing to end his persecutions."

George was elated. With such a huge potential win for Christianity by fulfilling this task, George's fear turned into resolve. "Consider it done!" he said with conviction.

George grasped his shield and mounted his winged horse. Pulling back on the reins, Ascalon reared up, and then bolted forward, as George bellowed, "Off we go to victory!"

For six hours, six minutes and six seconds, George galloped and flew through the countryside, covering miles of terrain, yet seeing no sign of Satan. However, he had stopped at three villages along the way, where the town's folk described the warrior in detail, even mentioning his special razor-sharp blade on his helmet, which he also used with deadly skill. His name was Malus, and he was roundly viewed as Satan's greatest warrior. The many tales they told of his ruthless massacres throughout the land were even hard for them to repeat, but even more troubling was the fact that they felt helpless, stating: "No mortal could ever prevail over Malus' diabolical strength and cruelty."

Such words further fueled George's resolve to annihilate this notorious demon, and he took flight, once again, to continue his search, this time with even greater zeal. An hour later, George's eyes bulged. He could see Malus on a rampage on an adjacent mountaintop, separated by a cavernous gap in the canyon with a lush valley below.

George gasped, as the armored devil swooped down on his red steed at a woman and her daughter and decapitated the mother, while his crimson beast impaled the young girl with its horns. Upon finishing this dastardly deed, Malus looked up and noticed George on the adjacent cliff.

The bat-winged red horse reared up, as the metal-clad warrior squealed like a rabid boar and charged toward the cliff. In response, George kicked the loins of Ascalon and charged toward the edge of his cliff. Soon both winged steeds jumped off and rose up into the air, high above the valley thousands of feet below.

As the aerial battle ensued, George wielded his sword and slashed at the devil-horse's bat wings, clipping off a section of patagium, thus partially crippling the horse's ability to fly. Being in close range, Malus, now in a fit of rage, leaned into George and used the razor sharp blade on his helmet to slice a gash in George's arm.

George lost control of Ascalon, and they began to spiral down the canyon toward the river below. The red demon horse shrieked a terrifying battle cry and followed in hot pursuit, this time puncturing Ascalon's hindquarters with its two sharp horns. Ascalon squealed in pain, igniting the ire of George, who despised the harm to his steed more than to himself. Suddenly a beam of light shone down, almost blinding George with the power of the Lord. He spun around swiftly, and with God's grace, he slashed the scarlet horse's wings once again, this time slicing one wing completely off!

The demonic warrior and his bleeding steed spiraled down helplessly and crashed into the craggy rocks on the banks of the river. George flew down to inspect the kill, and sighed with relief, Malus and his demon steed were both dead. With nightfall upon them, George rode into the skies and began his return.

As dawn broke, on February 23, 303 AD, George landed at Diocletian's villa. He tethered Ascalon to a post, then inspected Ascalon's and his own wounds. Miraculously they were both completely healed. Elated, he looked up and crossed himself. Then he strolled up to the entrance, where he met a guard. He was granted admission into the imperial palace and was greeted warmly by Diocletian, whose wife Prisca and two fellow praetorian guards all cordially offered their greetings, as well.

George knelt before the emperor, then stood up with a prideful grin. "Imperator, I have done as you asked. The demon warrior and his flying beast have been slain."

Yet, George squinted. He expected a grin in return, along with a reprieve for his fellow Christians, but Diocletian's face was firm like a chunk of granite. Perplexed, George added, "Does this not please you?"

The emperor responded with a question. "You said demon warrior, *not* Satan. Why?"

George sighed. "Well, yes, it was not Satan himself, but it was indeed his most terrifying warrior, a demon called Malus. I saw with my own eyes how he ruthlessly killed an innocent woman and her daughter. And he was, without question, the villain whom Romans feared most; as they informed me of his beastly steed and that he wore a special deadly helmet. The very same demon warrior and crimson horse you described, with bat wings."

Diocletian's lips twisted, semi impressed, as he glanced at his wife Prisca, who tepidly nodded her approval. He looked back at George. "Well, in that case, the death of an evil wretch is welcome news," he said flatly.

Again George squinted, as he glanced at Prisca, then back at the emperor. "But you said if I killed this demon that you would honor and defend Christians, yet you have not mentioned this. Why?"

Diocletian waved to his two praetorian guards. "Seize him!"

As they grabbed George vehemently by his arms, George bellowed, "Wait! What's going on!?"

With imperial gravity, Diocletian stepped closer. "My pact was that you must kill Satan. But you have only killed one devil among an army of demons. Malus might have been the most notorious demon, but they are all just minions to your ultimate Christian enemy, Satan." Diocletian shook his head, annoyed, as he added, "Romans never even heard of this evil king of Hell until you Christians infected our empire. Therefore, my empire is still threatened by him and his satanic devils that attack us, and it is all because of your troublesome Christian cult. So, this Satan of yours is the head of the snake, and he is the one that must be eliminated."

Prisca stepped forward and grasped Diocletian's arm, then whispered in his ear. The emperor then looked back at the brave warrior before him and sighed. Influenced by Prisca, Diocletian had second thoughts. Despite their disappointment, a praetorian warrior of his caliber would certainly be an asset, and he decided to make an offer. "However, I will set you free, George, *if* you recant being a Christian."

George vigorously shook his head. "No! Never!"

Diocletian snarled. "If it's a dead Christian martyr you choose to be, rather than an asset to Rome, so be it!" He glanced at his guards and barked, "Away with him!"

George was briskly taken away and escorted to prison.

Enraged, Diocletian summoned his own minions and ordered that the newly built Christian church in Nicomedia be razed and its scriptures burned. The next day, on February 24, he published his *Edict of the Christians*, thereby setting in motion the organized burning of Christian churches throughout the empire. Emboldened by Diocletian's *Edict*, Galerius' persecutions continued.

Two months later, on April 23, 303 AD, George was executed, thus fulfilling his religious commitment to become a martyr. However, attaining sainthood, Saint George's martyrdom would give way to an astonishing chain of events.

The persecutions of Christians were proving to be ineffective as even pagans were sick of the gory executions. Then Diocletian shocked all, once again, by peacefully retiring from his reign two years later on May 1, 305 AD, something no emperor had ever done. Then, a year later, on July 25, 306 AD, Constantine the Great would become a Caesar and eventually wrest control from Diocletian's legacy, the Tetrarchy. As sole emperor, Constantine instated Christianity as the exclusive religion of the Roman Empire, thereby seizing pagan temples and converting them to Christian churches and funding only bishops. Moreover, Constantine granted bishops judicial powers in certain legal cases and many perks unheard of for clergymen. As such, Christianity's rise and ultimate dominance in Western civilization was assured.

+ + + + +

Despite this tale's fictional battle, with Malus and winged horses, to this day, many nations celebrate Saint George on April 23, as the valiant warrior's legacy of slaying a dragon in Libya, as mentioned herein, lives on, regardless of a sheer lack of evidence.

PAINE AND THE GRANDEST ILLUSION

A frigid breeze sprinkled snowflakes across the streets of Paris, as a stagecoach carrying Thomas Paine arrived at White's Hotel, a hangout for mostly British and American subjects, who either couldn't speak French, like Thomas, or just enjoyed the English brew served on tap at its quaint tavern.

Paine had the honor of being invited to serve as a deputy in the French National Convention. France was in the midst of monumental turmoil, and as such the French embraced Paine's powerful words in his pamphlets *Common Sense* and *The American Crisis*, which fueled America's War for Independence, as well as his more recent *The Rights of Man*, which defended France's rights to demand freedom from tyranny. As such, they had every intention of throwing off the chains of monarchy and embracing a republican constitution. Thus, they welcomed the British born wordsmith, who had also attained U.S. citizenship, with open arms.

It was Christmas Eve of 1793, and Thomas had traveled from his new residence in Saint-Denis, just outside the city, to the hotel to celebrate finishing the first part of his latest work, *The Age of Reason*, his most provocative work to date.

Paine mingled with old friends from England and America, as well as with a handful of French politicians he had befriended at the seat of government. Many clamored to the celebrity's side, eager to hear his tales of historic merit and interactions with his entourage of famous friends, including George Washington, Thomas Jefferson, Benjamin Franklin, and other Americans, as well as admired Frenchmen like Lafayette. After several hours of meaningful conversations about politics with friends, Paine was too tired to travel back to the suburbs and decided to take a hotel room upstairs.

Exhausted, the fifty-five year old literary icon struggled to take off his clothes. He looked in the mirror, barely recognizing the tired old man standing before him, and yawned. However, despite all the adulation and fame, Thomas knew who he was, what he looked like, and what he believed in, and had no problem with any of that; he was a common man with common sense and a big mouth who didn't care if others rebuked him, as he was dedicated to liberty, equality, ethics and the truth. And for those who mocked his disheveled looks, with his sloppy hair, large nose and well-worn shirts and trousers, he knew the best part of an apple pie wasn't the dry outer crust, it was the rich filling inside.

Slipping under the blanket, he leaned over and blew out the candle. A cold wind rattled the windowpanes and seeped through the cracks, sending a chill through the air, while the small fireplace in the corner smoldered. Thirty minutes later, he had fallen into a deep slumber as his bulbous nose wheezed and whistled a snoring tune.

At an hour past midnight, his door rattled to the thunderous sound of fists on wood. Jolted upright, Paine shook his head, attempting to restart his mind, as stern voices in French pierced through the door and into his ears like rapiers. Still half asleep, he groggily rose out of bed and shuffled to the door. In the dark he could barely see the handle, but finally unlocked it.

At the door were two security agents and the hotel manager, who translated the bewildering news; he was under arrest!

Paine squinted. "I don't understand. This must be a mistake. I'm a deputy in the French government."

The French guards rolled their eyes and looked at the hotel manger for the translation. Yet what they heard offered no help, as they brutishly grabbed Paine's arm and attempted to drag him out.

Paine protested. "Halt!" He looked at the hotel manager. "Tell them I will comply, but they must allow me to get dressed."

What transpired over the next three days confounded and humiliated Paine. The agents had demanded to see his political works, and Paine directed them to his friend Joel Barlow, who only revealed a scant 31 pages worth of material, which didn't satisfy the officers. As such, they searched the premises, but found nothing. That was Paine's plan, as he didn't wish for them to find the mother lode he had stashed at his residence, unsure of what their ultimate objective was.

But that dead end didn't satisfy them, and off to Paine's residence in Saint-Denis they went. Finding his full set of writings, they rummaged through the papers but realized they contained nothing politically seditious in nature.

Regardless, the officers placed Paine in a *fourgons* and carted him to the Luxembourg Palace, which had recently been turned into a prison. The Committee of Public Safety, dominated by the radical Jacobins faction, was in full throttle arresting and imprisoning political enemies of the state and commoners charged with conspiracy.

Paine, and his fellow Girondins, who had moderate views and sought a republican constitution, now found themselves as potential enemies of the state. Worse yet, beyond the arrests were frightening stories of politicians with opposing views being executed without trials.

As Paine was escorted to the palace entrance he was disoriented by the bizarre paradox; namely, that such a gorgeous palace was being used as a prison. To him it mirrored how the beautiful nation of France was likewise being turned into a shameful prison by the Jacobins.

Compounding these depressing thoughts of the mayhem in Paris was when he saw his prison cell; it was a small room on the first floor that had been neglected for decades, thus it was dank and dreary. Its plaster walls were cracked and pealing from moisture and its brick floor was spotted with small puddles and mold from the thawing snow outside that seeped in.

To Paine's chagrin, his incarceration, which he thought would be a few days, turned into months. The only consolation was that he was allowed to roam the palace during daylight hours, and was entitled to buy newspapers. The latter being a saving grace for Paine, as keeping up with the political temperature in France and the world was of great interest to the worldly philosopher.

The huge dinning hall in the palace was setup with rows of tables for the prisoners, and on a sunny afternoon in April, Paine was sitting by himself having his lunch.

Just then, a new prisoner walked up, carrying a piece of bread and a cup of water, and asked in English, "Would you mind if I take this vacant seat next to you?"

Paine looked up at the man of about thirty-five years of age with a goatee and spectacles. "Not at all, it's not taken."

The man sat down, and said, "My name is Ernest Vérité."

"And I am Thomas Paine."

"Oh, yes, I knew that. Word gets around quick," Vérité said. "I've read about you in the papers, but had no idea what you looked like, until one of the guards pointed you out."

Paine sighed, hoping this new inmate wasn't going to be an irritable celebrity leech, which was one of the pangs of being famous. Yet being that the man radiated a pleasant demeanor and spoke English, he decided to give the

Frenchman the benefit of the doubt. "I imagine you would have never guessed that an old man, with a face like *this*, was the Thomas Paine of notoriety?"

Vérité laughed. "I'm pleased to see you have a sense of humor. It seems many of high esteem are often pompous windbags."

"Well, there's no pomp between us," Paine replied wittily.

Once again, Vérité laughed as he rubbed his goatee and then drew his chair in closer. "I'm honored to meet you. I must admit, I have read a few pages of your *Common Sense*, and I figured you to be a commonly good soul."

"That's very much appreciated, Monsieur Vérité."

Vérité squinted. "So I imagine you are a… religious man?"

"Well, as you gathered, *Common Sense* was a political work in defense of America declaring independence from my homeland, England. But I had become an American citizen and now I've been honored with French citizenship, as well. So as for me, my country is the world, and my religion is simply to do good."

"Ah, a man of the world," Vérité said thoughtfully. "An interesting concept, after all, we are all born into a nation or tribe, and in turn, take on that heredity as being who we are. When in reality, we are all just humans living on the same planet."

"Indeed we are," Paine replied, pleased that this inmate was proving to be a good conversationalist.

"And I agree wholeheartedly with your religion," Vérité said, "as I feel every man should live by that simple and benevolent advice. Personally, although I despise the Jacobins, I do agree with them and Voltaire on the topic of religion. There is no God, he was created by ancient men with vivid imaginations."

Paine's left eyebrow rose. "Well, I can fully understand your reasoning, Monsieur Vérité, especially considering the poor examples mankind has offered us since the beginning of time. Horus, Ra, Zeus, Odin, Gaia, Dagda, Brahma, Buddha, and the myriad of cults, like Mithraism and Zoroastrianism, which only proved to be lightweights when compared to the successful brainwashing of Judaism and Christianity."

Vérité shook his head. "I must confess, I didn't even know half of those pagan names. Once I abandoned the absurdities of the Judeo/Christian cult I focused my life on the pursuit of things that are *real* in nature and of *real* value to mankind; namely, chemistry or alchemy." Vérité reached over to officially greet Paine with a handshake. "And please, you may call me Ernest."

Paine nodded. "Ernest it is. And in earnest I shall try to remember that." As both men chuckled, Paine continued, "But your pursuits in chemistry will indeed reap better rewards, Ernest, for society and your own sanity. However, allow me to clarify my own stance on religion. You see, I'm a Deist. Which means I do believe in a God. Just not the false old man with a gray beard conjured up by the ancient Hebrews, who had temper tantrums and razed entire cities of men, women and children with brimstone and fire, or the more even-tempered version of him transformed by the Christians." Paine sniggered. "It appears their God has a split personality."

Ernest chuckled. "Yes, I never truly could relate to either version, but especially that hostile brute the Hebrews adored with such reverence and of course fear." He adjusted his glasses, and added with a chuckle, "Yes, they do seem to thrive on fear and destruction. Don't they?"

Paine nodded thoughtfully. "Yes, of course, *fear*. It's rather odd. The Hebrews control their flock with fear, much more so than with love." He paused as his eyes rolled in thought. "It reminds me of what Machiavelli said. 'It is better to be feared than loved.' Let's face it, such savage advice may have suited the unlawful world of Renaissance power lords or the Hebrew High Priests, but my philosophy runs counter to that, as it is founded upon the principles of being civilized and humane. In essence, administered with fairness and love. Progress depends on learning from our past, Ernest, and primitive tactics of fear should no longer be taught or tolerated."

Just then a guard strolled by, scrutinizing their every move. It was clear he was making sure they weren't plotting any schemes, being well informed that every prisoner there was a seditious rebel and a danger to the state.

Ernest frowned as he glanced at the guard, who now passed by. "I'm afraid fear is the new order of the day in France, Thomas."

Paine coughed and rubbed his ailing chest. The months of living in his damp and moldy cell room was taking its toll. He looked furtively left and right, then back at Vérité. Leaning closer, he whispered, "But you say you delve into alchemy. By chance, is there any special magic that can absolve us of this wrongful incarceration?"

Unexpectedly, Vérité rose to his feet and chuckled. "Magic!? No. Alchemy is scientific, Mr. Paine. I'm aware that others have besmirched my good profession, but I take great pride in my work." Discreetly, he motioned to Paine to take a stroll down a vacant corridor for privacy.

The palace corridor was garishly ornate, with gold leaf moldings and frescos, flanked by a series of large windows, and featured a variety of colorful perennials in decorative urns.

As the two men strolled along, Vérité's eyes scrutinized the various species. "You know, it's amazing what chemicals come from nature, from deep within the Earth or even from various plants and flowers, like these."

Paine shrugged. "I wouldn't know. The only trades I ever knew were when I designed an iron bridge that was never built, or was a staymaker, having followed in my father's footsteps many years ago."

Vérité looked at Paine quizzically and laughed. "Excuse me, I don't wish to be rude. But I just can't fancy you making corsets for women."

Paine glanced at Ernest and couldn't help but laugh, as well. "Yes, yes, of course. Most people likewise find it quite odd." His face withered to a solemn pout as his shoulders slumped. "Yet there are others who take great pleasure in ridiculing my lowbrowed past, Ernest. Heathens. All of them!"

Vérité's smile likewise withered to a somber picture of regret. "I do apologize. But, fear not. I, too, have little in the way of impressive ancestors to boast of. Take heed! We are self-made men, Thomas. And there's no shame in that."

Paine looked at his new prison mate with gratitude. "Why, thank you, Monsieur Vérité. I, of all people, should remember that." As he continued walking, his shoulders raised and his chest now inflated with pride. "My whole adult life has been devoted to inventing new political systems to offer liberty and equality for all." Spotting a beautiful red rose, Paine stopped, leaned over and plucked it free. As he took a sniff, a thorn pricked his finger. With a wince, he sucked his bloody finger, and added, "It's just that once you fall in with men of great stature, and walk in their shoes, you soon realize that their bloody shoes don't truly fit that well. I guess you can say, I do feel a bit out-of-step with them at times."

As they resumed walking down the corridor, Paine continued, "But, by George, I do know that my mind can fill just as large a hat as any of them." Taking another sniff of the rose, he added, "And damn them all! To obtain beauty one must endure some pain. And in that endeavor, I am ready, and so, too, must they be ready; after all, Paine's my name!" With a coy smile he concluded, "So my voice shall always be a clarion call for the common man as I harangue every pompous and royal windbag with Common Sense!"

Vérité burst out with a guffaw! "And your splendid sense of humor and wit is rather uncommon among your haughty ilk, Mr. Paine. Well said, well said indeed!"

"Dear me," Paine said, as he tossed the rose into an empty urn. "We've veered off topic." He gazed around, then back at Ernest. Again he whispered, "If you truly are an alchemist, have you concocted anything of practical use?"

"Indeed, I have," he whispered back. "I've mastered several new compounds with rather stunning results." With a playful face, he added in an English accent, "In fact, even a jolly good ointment for that bloody finger of yours."

As Paine giggled, Ernest added, "I do hope I used your bloody British accent properly?"

Paine nodded. "That you have, Monsieur Vérité. For who am I to complain when I'm an appointed French official who can't speak French?" Regaining a serious bearing, he whispered, "But tell me, is any one of those concoctions of significant use to us here, and now?"

Vérité nodded furtively. "Oh, yes, Mister Paine," he replied with a professional bearing. "I've been working on this one particular formula for quite some time now. And it *is* truly extraordinary."

"Well, pray tell!" Paine beseeched him.

Just then a loud commotion erupted as two guards dragged a prisoner through a nearby corridor toward the palace exit. Paine and Vérité looked on with trepidation as one of the guards beat the man with the butt end of his firearm.

The man screamed in French, "I will not go to the gallows! You're barbarians! All of you! France has gone mad!"

"And mad I am," yelled the irate guard. "Mad that traitorous maggots, like *you*, defile this great nation. Off with your head, Monsieur *Traitre*!"

With a desperate punch to the guard's stomach, and an elbow to the other, the prisoner broke free and started to run. The malicious guard aimed his pistol and pulled the trigger. With a harrowing pop, the prisoner fell face-first on the opulent marble floor, which echoed throughout the palace. The cruel guard walked ominously toward his fallen prey, and as the man wriggled on the floor, he kicked him with his shinny black boot, thus rolling the man onto his back. As a pool of blood spread across the tessellated floor, the man uttered, "You bastard! Go ahead, finish it. I prefer to be dead, just as France is dead."

With that, the guard fired the fatal shot straight to the man's head. Maurice, the other guard, scurried over. "Jacque! Look what you've done!"

Jacque gazed at his fellow officer with intense malice, yet Maurice laughed, and said, "You made a mess of Marie de Medici's beautiful marble floor."

Jacque managed to chuckle, but his lugubrious scowl reclaimed his murderous face. "I'm really in no mood for levity, Maurice. Get the janitor to clean this rubbish up." He then turned, noticing Thomas and Ernest. "What are you two looking at?"

Vérité choked on his words, "Ah, oh, noth... abso... lutely nothing, sir."

"It damned well better be nothing, you seditious little rodent!"

Trembling, Ernest gazed sheepishly downward. "Yes, s-sir."

Maurice called out, "Best you two go to your cell rooms, *at once!*"

Thomas and Ernest made an about-face and walked timidly hunchbacked toward their rooms. Once far enough away, Vérité uttered nervously, "I guess we'll discuss my potion tomorrow."

Paine nodded, then stopped as he reached his door. "Till the morrow it is, Ernest. Try to forget what we just saw, and have yourself a good night." With a nod from Ernest, Paine grasped the door handle and entered his makeshift cell.

Paine covered his large nose with his handkerchief as the dank and moldy brick floor emanated moisture and spores that rankled his lungs. Suppressing cough after cough, Thomas wiped his nose and clutched his aching chest as he undressed and tossed his clothes haphazardly on the nearby table. He gazed at the old and rigid army cot and sighed. It never allowed him a sound sleep, yet as an obedient victim of his fate, he crawled onto the flimsy canvas material and accepted his fate, once again.

Thoughts ran through his head. He couldn't believe the course his life had taken him. From being the most prominent literary voice in the War for Independence in America, and befriending men like Washington, Jefferson and others, to becoming an honorary citizen and political officer in France, Paine had been amazed and proud of his critical contributions to world history.

To a much lesser extent, he accepted his rise to fame as an inevitable perk of his high station in life. For he knew his reward was earned by merit, not heredity, just like how he despised the monarchy, based on a hereditary bloodline, with no qualifications necessary. That's why he knew it was imperative to dedicate his efforts to making the French monarchy a relic of the past. And that meant even if he had to endure the frightening hardship of being detained in a prison and suffering poor health. A French Republic had to come to fruition. That he believed fervently. Not only for the French people, but also to serve as a beacon in the very heart of Europe, one that would cause neighboring monarchs to likewise fall like dominos.

Lying on his back, Paine's eyes gazed up at the decorative ceiling as his candle's light burned dimmer and dimmer. Despite his eyes growing heavy, the night proved to be extremely difficult for him, and every prisoner, to fall asleep. For it wasn't only thoughts of the brutal murder earlier that kept him awake. Throughout the night, at various intervals, they could hear prisoners moaning or squealing in agony, either being beaten for sadistic pleasure or dragged out into carriages to be carted off to the guillotine. What the newspapers called The Reign of Terror was escalating at a bloody and malignant pace, and Paine's nerves were being frayed, just like the pull cord on the overactive guillotine itself.

Beyond the current killing spree was the memory of the September Massacres last year. Jean-Paul Marat, among others, had advocated the execution of prisoners to prevent them from joining the Prussians. Their fear was that neighboring monarchs were going to help King Louis XVI from losing his throne. But alas, Jean-Paul Marat, only months later, was stabbed to death while in his bath. Charlotte Corday had claimed to be an informant with knowledge of the whereabouts of the hunted Girondins, and she was allowed into his bathing room. However, Charlotte was a Girondin sympathizer, and Marat's last minute of life was one of shock and horror. She was later caught and lost her head, but mayhem was escalating all across Paris.

Of even greater shock was the execution of King Louis XVI a year ago by guillotine. Despite Paine rallying to his defense, primarily due to the King's vital support of America's revolution, he eventually flipped allegiances. That was because the King had fled France, but was dragged back to answer for his private letters, which revealed he intended to eliminate all proposals for a constitutional government and remain a monarch in all matters of state. While the king's assassination shocked many, his wife's beheading nine months later added to the terror and chaos, as Marie Antoinette met the guillotine on October 16, 1793.

All in all, Thomas Paine had much on his mind, and sleep was a fleeting escape from the horrors that plagued him and every soul in France.

As shimmering vestiges of dawn passed through his room's small window, Paine's eyelids groggily strained to open. The mere three hours of sleep had only exacerbated his now infected lungs and achy muscles. He grasped his handkerchief and wiped his sweaty forehead, even though his room was cool and damp. A chill reverberated through his body as he shook his head with a shiver and sat upright.

His door swung open as a young guard stepped in. "Get up! It's time for your morning exercise walk," he demanded.

"I'm not feeling very well," Paine uttered. "Perhaps I'll skip the walk today."

"I don't care how you feel or what you wish, Monsieur! Get your arse up, or I *will* do it for you!"

Paine huffed and then rose unsteadily to his feet. With a cough gurgling with phlegm, he managed to say, "F-Fine. Please g-give me a minute to get dressed."

The strapping young guard, of a mere nineteen years of age, rolled his eyes. "Make it quick!" he barked, then stepped back into the corridor.

Paine's body and health had taken a turn for the worse as he struggled to get dressed. Paine was literally *in* pain. He wasn't sure which malady he had contracted, be it early stages of pneumonia or worse yet typhus, but all he knew was that his health was already breaking down and he had to find a way to get out of this dank prison palace somehow. That's why he needed to speak to Ernest Vérité, once again, in hopes that the alchemist concocted some type of magical potion that could perhaps drug the guards or give them some sort of magical power to escape.

"Move it!" blasted the irritable guard, who had reentered the room and now stood right behind him.

Paine nearly jumped out of his shoes, as he spun around. "I'm ready," he said calmly, having always been compliant with the law, even when ruffians perverted it.

To Paine's chagrin, the brawny young guard physically escorted Paine throughout the palace at a quick pace, which he tried to keep up with, yet the minutes turned to over an hour and seemed longer than usual. Exhausted, Paine almost collapsed, as he pleaded for the fourth time. "Please, I need a moment to rest. As I told you, I'm feeling very sick."

The guard grunted, equally exhausted. Not by the strenuous exercise but by Paine's annoying complaints. Luckily it was due to Paine's courteous nature that the wordsmith didn't get a brutal beating, and the young guard complied. "Very well, old man. Take a rest. But don't go far. I'll be right *here*, waiting."

Paine stepped inside one of the palace galleries nearby and sat on an ornate bench. The gallery was still partially dim as the dawn's rays had yet to illuminate the large room, and only two wall-hung candles had been lit. Trying to recapture his breath, he gazed solemnly at the parquet floor. His mind still couldn't fathom why the radical Jacobins viciously refused the enlightenment of building a republic. And his incarceration in a century-old dank prison, even if beautiful in its architectural splendor, was only destroying his health.

Moreover, with this teenaged guard wearing him down, Paine wondered if that, too, was part of their plot. Every day he witnessed more and more of his friends and sympathizers for a republic being led to the gallows or beaten to death by the thousands. He wondered, *Was this dank old prison part of the plan to silence me, a public figure, by natural causes, compounded by this young guard wearing me down to the point of a heart attack?*

Just then, Paine thought he might have a heart attack! Not by the over exertion, but by what his eyes were now honored to behold. Adorning the twenty-two-foot high walls were a series of twenty-four huge paintings by Peter Paul Rubens.

Paine was transfixed by the gargantuan display of gargantuan talent by Rubens and the gargantuan prestige and power that Marie de Medici had wielded.

The all-powerful Medici family had strategically exported Marie from Florence to France with a special mission, just as they had Catherine decades earlier. And that was to subtly infiltrate and dominate France by marriage, which both Italian women achieved with much success.

Marie had married King Henry IV, who shared her love for the arts. It was Henry, with Marie's insistence, who added the largest wing to the Louvre with the extra novelty of allowing artists to utilize the first floor to advance their own skills. Meanwhile, Marie commissioned Rubens to paint a series of paintings dedicated to *her* achievements.

As Paine sat in awe of Rubens's monumental canvases, his mind veered from Marie to King Henry IV. He now recalled how Henry lived through turbulent times, as new rebellious offshoots of the Christian religion had collided, and brutal massacres stained the once monolithic enterprise. Roman Catholics, who once held complete control of their religion, were forced to contend with violent Calvinists, Huguenots, Lutherans, Protestants, Anglicans, Puritans, Quakers and more.

Visions of all these Christian factions fighting and killing one another colored Paine's mind with ominous shades of crimson red. And the fact that a Catholic zealot had stabbed and killed King Henry put the final bloody brushstroke on Paine's gory vision of the homicidal hypocrisy of religion. He shook his head, appalled at the folly of mankind for its fanaticism over the manmade rules of dogma, and the convoluted tales of a one and only Hebrew God illogically transformed by Christians into a Trinity.

The young guard barked, 'Times up! Let's go, old man."

Startled, Paine spun around and rose to his feet. "I must ask you, have you been tasked with driving me to my grave?"

"Not yet, old man. But if ordered to do so, expect to draw your last breath," the young guard retorted, being only one of thousands of teens inculcated with blind militancy without morals.

"Must you always remind me of my old age? I'm aware that I'm old, and you are very fortunate to be young. You have a full life ahead of you. But, please, son, I would genuinely appreciate if you called me Thomas, and show a little compassion for your fellow man," Paine said, in an attempt to temper the boy's belligerence.

"And I would appreciate you following orders without any back lip!" he growled. "Now, let's go! *Old man!*"

Paine seethed internally. And without a word, he complied and suffered another hour of pain, pushing his sick body up and down large flights of stairs, down long corridors, and passing the dinning hall, yet without permission to stop.

Finally, the guard glanced at the large clock on the wall and grunted, "Time for breakfast, old man."

For once, Paine glared at the guard with disdain. Over the past two hours he had gotten fed up with this spoiled and misguided youth's coarse ways and inhumane treatment. These were all things Paine believed would evaporate once a fair government was instated, one that would enact legislation on behalf of its citizens to allow free enterprise to bolster productivity, enhance education with knowledge and morals, and eliminate poverty, all, to some degree, being the reasons why the disenchanted had noxious behaviors and committed violent crimes.

Burdening Paine's weary mind even more was the recent decree that he would no longer be allowed to purchase newspapers, which was his lifeline to the daily events of the world outside. As a man of letters, reading the paper was like drinking water. It was crucial to his very existence. With the Reign of Terror spreading all across France, and the Angel of Death strolling the prison's halls, Paine was starting to seriously fear for his life.

Compounding those fears was the fact the he had been writing letters to Gouverneur Morris, American Minister to France, pleading to speak on his behalf to secure his release. One of the roadblocks had been that the French were declaring Paine to be a British citizen, thus being an enemy of the state. Paine had responded that he was an American, thus being an ally of France, and should be released immediately. Furthermore, Paine had been granted honorary citizenship in France when he was appointed Deputy of the National Convention, thus serving in their very government. Yet all that didn't seem to matter, as even the letters he had previously sent to his good friend, President George Washington, elicited only strange silence.

And looking at the young belligerent guard before him, Paine likewise chose silence, as he marched into the dinning hall and was served his meager portion of hard bread, a hard-boiled egg, and a glass of water. As he sat down at one of the tables with four other inmates, he scanned the hall for Ernest Vérité. But to his chagrin, he was nowhere to be seen. Worriedly, Paine's mind feared the worst.

Worse yet, months passed, and in tandem with Paine's debilitating ailments was his devastating assumption that the Angel of Death must have dragged Ernest away in the middle of the night to that hideous death machine, the guillotine.

The perpetual negative responses from Gouverneur Morris and continued silence from his once good friend, George Washington, weighed heavily on his distressed mind. He couldn't believe that his fellow Americans, whom he had given so much to help achieve a political miracle, had abandoned him. Over the past few weeks, Paine's health had deteriorated drastically, putting him in a state of depression. As such, he was allotted time to convalesce in his cell room, which proved to make matters worse.

It was now midnight in July of 1794, and Paine swung open and outward his cell door. Peering down the dark corridor, he could vaguely see a suspicious figure at the far end of the hallway. Slowly walking past every door, the dark figure approached closer and closer. Paine's heart raced as he envisioned it to be the Angel of Death stalking its next victim, when suddenly the apparition came before him!

With the candle now lighting the elderly guard's face, he said, "It's late, Monsieur. Go back to bed." And he simply continued making his rounds.

Paine clutched his chest with his shaking hands, relieved. Then obediently, he went to bed. The next day Paine was elated to find out that he was allowed to have visitors again, and several old friends stopped by. They spent the whole day in Paine's room; giving the political prisoner much needed encouragement to help his ailing body, mind and soul. It was the best tonic he could ever have wished for. But the hour had gotten late, and all visitors were instructed to leave. Having left his cell door wide open all day, he closed the door and once again went to bed, this time with a much clearer mind and his hopes slightly lifted.

At the break of dawn, Paine was awakened by screams and skirmishes in the corridor. He was well aware that jailers came at midnight or just before dawn to collect the next round of prisoners destined for the gallows. As such, with much foreboding, he resigned himself to the inevitable and leaned back, waiting to see if his door would be next. As cries of terrified prisoners arose and then faded, along with their lives, Paine's stomach turned with each harrowing minute that passed.

After twenty minutes, however, the almost daily exercise of murder had finally subsided. Paine closed his eyes with relief, when suddenly his door swung open! Paine's eyes widened with utter shock! It was Ernest Vérité!

"My god!" Ernest said. "You not only look awful, you look like you saw a ghost."

Paine sprung to his feet with a wobble and embraced his dear friend. "I'm so glad to see you. And a ghost, indeed, I thought they, well, you know, carted you off."

Ernest glanced at the inside of Paine's door, noticing a chalk mark. Now *his* heart raced. "Thomas, what's this mark doing on the inside of your door? It's supposed to be on the outside. That means you were selected to be..." Nervously, he peered behind him to see if anyone was there, and with the corridor vacant, he swiftly closed the door. He pulled a handkerchief out of his pocket and began scrubbing the chalk off the door.

Paine squinted, not having even noticed the chalk mark. "Dear me, I was with some friends yesterday, and the door was left open. I guess the executioner marked the inside by mistake." A white flash clouded his eyes, as his face went flush. "Oh, my, the Angel of Death *did* come for me!"

Having cleaned off the death mark, Ernest spun around, relieved. "Indeed he had. Even though angels don't exist."

Paine squinted, then chuckled. "Ah, yes, of course. You have an enlightened mind, Ernest."

"Well, we both do when it comes to religious fairytales, but you were extremely lucky. You should have been lying on the bed of the guillotine by now, with your head in a basket." He adjusted his glasses and peered back at the door, making sure the death mark was sufficiently cleaned off with no telltale signs. Contented, he looked back at his fortunate friend. "I'm sorry they never told you of my whereabouts, but they actually released me in the middle of the night. I, too, was terrified, thinking it was my last ride on Earth, until they arrived at my laboratory. Evidently, a friend of mine had spoken on my behalf to a local judge, who ordered my release with the proviso that I don't make contact with any of the prisoners I met here. However, not one to follow orders, I just had to see you."

"Thank you, my good friend. And I'm elated that you managed to secure your liberty. That's splendid news. I was seriously melancholy, having believed you were dead. But what criteria did your friend utilize to attain such a pardon?"

Ernest sat down at the table and pulled a small vial of liquid out of his pocket and placed it on the table.

Paine squinted. "They released you for *that*?"

Ernest laughed. "No, not this. Believe it or not, they released me for a special lubricant I invented."

"Lubricant. For what?"

Ernest frowned. "Well, that part I'm honestly not happy about." He paused, then uttered, "Its used on the pulleys of guillotines."

Paine closed his eyes for an agonizing moment, then opened them. "That truly is disturbing, Ernest."

"I hope you can do me the favor of never mentioning it to anyone. The thought of having any connection to that ghastly machine is one of those Faustian deals one makes with the devil."

Paine nodded solemnly, knowing Ernst did what he had to in order to stay alive. Gazing back at his friend, he quipped, "But as you and I know, there is no such thing as the devil. So your deal was just pure pragmatism."

Ernest's somber face morphed into grin. "I'm so glad to see your wondrous wit is still alive and well."

Paine smiled. "Well my wit might be alive and well, but my health is another matter."

"Well, this little vial I have here might give you something to at least give your mind some exercise."

Paine walked closer and sat at the table beside him, as Ernest said, "This extraordinary mixture is my ultimate invention, Thomas."

"Well, go on!" Paine pressed, having been eager to hear about this liquid for months. "What is it for?"

Ernest smiled. "Mind travel. At first, taking a single spoonful gave me colorful dreams and illusions. But after careful analysis and continued corrections, I began to realize that my thoughts, while drinking this elixir, generated vivid scenes of past experiences once I fell asleep."

Paine laughed. "So you created an elixir, a love potion? Does it generate love stories of the past, such as Romeo and Juliet?"

Ernest frowned, not appreciating jokes about his hard work and creating something humankind never even thought possible. "Make fun all you like, Thomas, but I call it an elixir because I really have fallen in love with it, and its astonishing capabilities. Moreover, with some additional refinements, I believe it will yield even more miraculous results."

Paine raised both hands in defense. "I apologize. My wit sometimes tramples etiquette. But just allay my fears that all this talk about miraculous results won't spiral into a farce like the miraculous events in religious texts?"

Ernest nodded. "I guarantee that, Thomas. And being that I'm an accomplished scientist, you must know that my elixir is nothing like a burning bush nor will it cure lepers or the blind."

"Well, in that case, I'm truly glad I'm not blind, because I'm ready to see what this potion can do."

Vérité pushed the vial toward Thomas. "This potion enables mind travel. Think hard of a person or place you'd like to visit, then drink it. It will make you fall into a deep sleep. I came to realize that the amount of potion determines the length of time one can explore the past. One vial, or shotglass full, enables a journey of fifteen minutes. And take heed; presently I know of no way of breaking the venture, hence also your slumber, once you're in it, for as I said, this puts you in a very deep sleep. Anyhow, chose your timing of when you take it and your options of where in the past you'd like to visit carefully. And you must concentrate very hard on the person or place to get the most accurate result."

Paine looked at the small vial, impressed and eager. "It's rather hard to believe this little bit of liquid can perform such a miracle." He looked up at Vérité. "You truly have entered the ranks of a god."

Ernest chuckled. "Mankind has underestimated itself since the beginning of time. Although I don't profess to be a god, there have been countless geniuses throughout history that have put mankind on an upward trajectory. The only sad part is that there have been far too few. Mankind has been plagued with a vast majority of mediocrity and only a very few savants per generation."

"Well, I'm honored to sit here with you."

"And I with you," Ernest replied.

Paine shook his head. "I'm no genius. Yes, I committed myself to reading the wisdom of others and building upon those ideas, but men like you or Newton are of a different ilk." He glanced down at the vial. "So I'm very eager to give this potion a test run."

Ernest looked surprised. "You mean now? This very minute." He glanced around the room. "In this prison?"

"Certainly. You said it lasts only fifteen minutes. Can you stand guard while I take the journey?"

"Well, I suppose so. I brought this just to show you, but I guess we can manage it here." He pointed to the cot. "Very well. Prepare yourself by laying down first, as the potion works quickly, and if standing, you might fall and hurt yourself." Vérité pushed the vial closer. "Go on. Give it a whirl. I'll stand watch."

With that, Paine grasped the vial and walked over to the cot. He situated himself on it and opened the vial. He glanced at Ernest "Here I go!" then he swallowed the tonic.

His eyes rolled in circles and he grasped his head, feeling a surge of blood as it rushed through his brain, igniting its neurons with electrical intensity. Closing his eyes, he was overcome by an eerie blackness that soon burst into a spectrum of vivid colors! Paine's hands instinctively grabbed the edges of the cot, as his illusive visions appeared to propel him through a spiraling corridor of colors. With his body now in a deep state of slumber, his mind grew hyperactive. Focusing his mind sharply on a previous event, the swirls of colors evaporated into a vivid scene of his past.

Standing before him was his dear old friend and general of the Continental Army, George Washington.

With astonishing clarity, Paine saw himself speaking with Washington about his pamphlets *Common Sense* and *The American Crisis* during their time together, just days before Valley Forge. The vision in his mind played the scene exactly as it occurred. However, Paine was viewing this event as an outsider, looking at himself in action as he interacted with Washington. The conversations and movements were indeed precise as was the location. The vivid reality of the moment did not appear like a painting on canvas one views, but rather he was in the moment itself, except for the fact that he was experiencing it from a different viewpoint, as if an invisible spectator.

The fifteen minutes passed quickly as Paine slowly emerged from his slumber. He opened his eyes to see Ernst standing before him. He sat up, a bit groggy, and shook his head. Blinking hard, he said, "Dear m-me, Ernest, my head aches. I f-feel as if I downed s-several pints of lager."

Ernest chuckled. "Ah, yes. I forgot to mention that. It's best that you drink plenty of water to flush the chemicals out of your system." Already prepared, Ernest handed Thomas a glass of water. "I'm sorry to add that it will take almost a half hour for the headache to dissipate."

Paine took a gulp and then said excitedly, "But, glory b-be, the journey was astonishing, Ernest! It's q-quite unfathomable, really." A grin enlivened his face. "An elixir it is. I am in l-love!"

As Ernest chuckled, Thomas added with a groggy slur, "F-furthermore, it was j-just as you s-said, Ernest. I willed myself to a time s-several years ago, and *presto!* I was there! I s-saw George Washington and m-myself during the war, j-just after he lost New York Harbor to the B-British. It was exact in every d-detail." He scratched his throbbing head, then looked deep into Vérité's eyes. "But I t-thought I would b-be reliving that experience? But, nay, I was only a-afforded the ability to observe."

Vérité nodded. "Yes. These visions only offer us the ability to view moments of the past, not interact with them or alter them." He pulled over a high-back chair and sat down next to him. He paused but a moment then added, "I have given this much thought, Thomas. You see, the mind game of time travel posses some very baffling questions and some serious concerns. Namely, if I were to change one single event, by intention or by folly, it would alter history and could cause catastrophic results." He interlocked his fingers, planted his elbows on the armrests, then rested his chin on his knuckles, as he said, "For instance: Imagine if you tried to stop General Howe from routing Washington's troops from Manhattan and Long Island. What then?"

Paine's checks swelled with a grin. "That w-would be grand, Ernest! The redcoats w-would have never controlled New York harbor or Long Island for the d-duration of the war. It would have been a s-sterling success, and one for me to g-glorify in print."

Ernest nodded solemnly with an erudite gaze. "Yes. I imagined you would say such a thing."

Thomas noticed the grim response, and queried, "I know you're an h-honorable Frenchman, but don't t-tell me you were a Tory s-sympathizer?"

Vérité unclenched his fingers and raised his head. With a chuckle he said, "No, no. As you Americans would say, 'I'm a full-blooded patriot to the very core.' I even fully endorsed Lafayette's great service to help you all win that war. So, no, Thomas, I would never have wished for the British monarchy to have succeeded."

Paine prided himself on being a logical thinker and was a tad annoyed with himself for not grasping the metaphysical nature of the conversation. He took another swig of water, thinking that perhaps the potion impeded more than his slurred speech, rather his brain from functioning properly, as he asked, "Very w-well. I'm a bit b-befuddled, Ernest. What did I s-say wrong? After all, a v-victory by Washington, securing Manhattan and Long Island, might have ended t-the war much sooner and saved c-countless lives."

To Paine's further befuddlement, Ernest nodded. "Yes, that's true."

Paine's head craned backward. "So, n-now you agree?"

Ernest shook his head. "No, I don't agree in this particular scenario, which would have altered history. I do agree that, yes, it would have been splendid to have gained another victory, but you failed to assess what could have happened if that was to be."

Paine was still befuddled, as he shook his titillating head. "Ernest, your w-word games are even more p-perplexing than your illusionary m-mind games. What, pray tell, are you t-trying to s-say?"

Vérité leaned back in his chair. "Thomas, yes, a victory of saving New York, at that moment, would have been greeted with much elation. But you must consider this; it was that devastating blunder that ignited the fireball of resolve in Washington's gut. And that was for him to do what no one in history had ever done. Crossing the icy Delaware River on Christmas night, in the bitter and frigid cold, and without proper supplies and clothing, Washington and his troops managed to score an astounding victory by overtaking the Hessians. It was indeed a miracle."

Paine once again shook his numb head, this time gaining a bit more clarity. A sigh emanated from his mouth as he contemplated Vérité's potent words.

"And, Thomas," Ernest continued, "It was your hallowed words in *The American Crisis* that energized those tired, starving and freezing soldiers to do the unthinkable. For it was Washington who ordered your pamphlet read to his troops. He knew they needed something he couldn't offer. For you proved that the pen is indeed mightier than the sword."

Paine filled up with emotion as a tear welled in his eye. The gravity and magnitude of that historic event, and his part in it, was one that was very dear to him.

Meanwhile, Ernest continued, "Yes, *your words*, my friend, 'These are the times that try men's souls.' And they would have never been written if not for the humiliating defeat of losing New York. So who knows what course the war would have taken without that essential inspiration? *Your* inspiration, as well, in this case."

Paine wiped away the tear; embarrassed more so for not being the stoic man he was than for not unraveling the consequences of manipulating time. He regained his manly bearing and said, "Ernest, you have proven yourself to be more than a mere alchemist, for you are a metaphysical scientist with an astonishingly analytical mind."

Vérité stood up. "Flattery from our era's most influential political mind is most welcome to fuel my own endeavors, Thomas, but your kind words are not entirely true. It's just that the potion has not completely worn off just yet, and that had you a bit disoriented." With a smile, he added. "Well, the hour is late and I must get something to eat so I may fuel my astonishingly analytical mind, as you say."

Paine smiled, but it quickly withered. "Must you leave so soon?"

"I'm afraid so," Ernest said. "I admit, it is hard for me to leave you, especially in this rotten place. But know this, Thomas. I only have two more vials in my pocket. And the chemicals I require for this solution are very rare and hard to obtain. So it might be a year or more until I can formulate more."

Paine's expression turned contemplative. "That seriously curtails my ambitions for this incredible p-potion, Ernest. But naturally, I wouldn't impose upon you for another dose until you can p-procure additional resources to manufacture more."

Vérité tapped his pocket. "I intended to give these to you, as well, Thomas. I don't need to take more of this potion myself. I already know its capabilities. My experiments henceforth will all be altering the mixture to see if I can achieve different results."

"And what different k-kinds of results do you seek?"

"Well, that's all part of experimentation, Thomas. Serendipity often plays a role in the art of invention. So, I'm not sure what else I can achieve with this particular elixir, but perhaps even longer journeys, or maybe something unexpected. Who knows?"

Paine smiled. "As you say, an elixir it is, for I love your thirst for it and for adventure."

"Well, I see your speech has already cleared up. So I imagine your wits have been restored faster than expected. The question for you now is; what time in history, or person, will you visit next?"

Paine pointed to his papers on the desk. "I've been writing my next book, the second part of my *Age of Reason*. So, I'm very focused on religion."

"I gather visiting Jesus is your next journey?"

Paine smiled. "Yes. I imagine believers, and even nonbelievers like us, would chose Jesus."

"Well, I can save you the trip. He indeed was one of my first attempts of a journey, but alas, nothing came of it."

Paine squinted. "What do you mean?"

"I guess you can say it was either divine intervention that prevented it, or the fact that there is no official document to record Jesus' birth. The Romans were very organized, and birth records and even census reports exist, yet none mention a Jesus of Nazareth."

Paine nodded thoughtfully. "Ah, yes, I see. So either the religious fanatics are right, or we are, as no records of an actual person yields a non-existent person or place to visit back in time."

"Exactly," Vérité said. "So, what is your next option?"

Paine rubbed his chin. "I reckon with only two vials leaving me two visitations I would have to opt first for Julian the Apostate."

Ernest's head recoiled. "Julian, the Eastern Roman Emperor? Why him?"

Paine smiled. "Yes, I imagine he would not spring onto most people's list, but being engrossed in my book on religion, and being of a political mindset, Julian is a very intriguing figure. His writings have been very scarce, since Christians did a fine job of either expunging them or hiding them where inquisitive minds couldn't get a hold of them. So it will be quite interesting to see what exactly the revisionist Christians sought to hide. And after that, my second journey shall be Emperor Titus."

Ernest glanced at the clock. "In that case, I suppose I can delay eating for an hour or so for you to take both journeys while I stand watch."

"Thank you, this means a great deal to me," Paine said excitedly.

Ernest extracted the vials from his pocket. "Oh, yes, I forgot to mention; one vial is larger than a shot glass, so you'll have more than fifteen minutes with that one."

Paine smiled. "That's splendid. In that case, I'll use the fifteen minute vial for Julian and save the longer one for Titus."

"So be it," Ernest said, as Paine readied himself on the cot and Ernest handed him the second of three vials.

Paine concentrated hard, then opened the vial and swallowed the liquid. He closed his eyes, and, once again, the blackness in his mind sprung-forth brilliant colors, which then morphed into a scene of a landscape with tents and populated with Roman soldiers setting up camp.

Paine was impressed, not only of arriving, but realizing that he had the capability of walking amid the dream of reality. As such, he walked through the campsite and marveled at seeing actual Roman soldiers wearing *lorca hamata* armor, with its chainmail construction, and sporting *berkasovo* helmets, having altered the popular *galea* helmet of pervious centuries.

Straight ahead, and some distance back, Paine spotted an ornate tent. It was large with sentries standing nearby. *That must be Julian's headquarters*, he thought, and he moved through the soldiers like a ghost and entered the tent.

Paine was thrilled beyond expectation. There, before him, sat Emperor Julian and his Praetorian Prefect of the East, Salutius, his most trusted right-hand man. Paine's heart beat faster. He had long dreamed of such things and here it was, he was there!

Julian slammed his gladius on the table, then spoke: "Salutius, I can't believe how these damn Persians have pushed us into a retreat!"

"None of us can, Imperator. But your previous victory of crossing the Tigris and pushing them back was flawless. As we know, battles are never solely to one side's benefit, and so today they managed to gain a small advantage. But I agree, it is wise that we'll be heading back to our own border tomorrow morning. We can regroup and replenish our men and our spirits."

Julian leaned back and sighed. "Yes, you're right, enough of this singular setback. Tomorrow is another day."

Just then a *drungarios* officer popped his head into the tent. "Imperator, we have a few Christians who are saying prayers. Should I admonish them?"

Julian's lips twisted. "No, by all means, let them find strength wherever they may, even if from a fable."

As the officer exited, Salutius said, "It appears some are not clear on your stance regarding religion. Myself included. I mean, of course I know you passed laws to reinstate our pantheon of gods, yet Constantine's edicts exclusively favored bishops and penalized all others. That's had dire consequences for our empire. Most of our temples have been converted into Catholic churches and I'm curious just how far you plan on going to correct this abomination?"

Julian stood up, unstrapped his *lorca hamata* and irritably tossed it aside. He groaned. "Yes, yes, I know. The problems with wars, and this irritating problem with religion; they're the two most polarizing and agonizing elements of humankind." He banged the table with his knuckles. "I have no intentions of eliminating other religions, Salutius, even the troublesome Christians or Jews. They have always been a plague upon us from their very inception. However, like the great Augustus, I believe the people have the right to worship whomever or whatever they wish, be it some old man in the ether or a human with a jackal's head. The problem is people are too gullible and too complacent to challenge their traditions, and that leaves the few with strategies and ambition seeking ways to control them. Or in the case of the Hebrews, those with vivid imaginations."

Salutius likewise took off his *lorca hamata* and set it in the ground. "Yes, I can understand how some are destined to rule and others follow, but as for allowing these foolish sheep to worship false gods only serves to separate and divide mankind and cause trouble. As for Augustus, he had good fortune, since the Jews inflamed tensions mostly after his reign, while the Christian cult didn't even exist then."

"True, but the Roman policy has always been one of tolerance and acceptance," Julian said with a sense of Roman pride. "We have embraced more religions in our empire than any other nation or tribe that ever inhabited the Earth. And I'm proud of that tradition. Some things are meant to stay intact, while others demand change. And it was Constantine who started this religious revolution, and I must try to subdue at least some of the damage he caused."

"Damage indeed!" Salutius replied with humiliation. "From the few things I have learned about this Christian cult I am baffled at how it has so many followers. Their beliefs are truly bizarre. I hear rumors that some are even cannibals, eating the body of Christ and they practice other barbaric rituals, as well. Yet based on the Hebrew god, whom I think they call Yahweh, this Christian sect also feels superior to everyone else on Earth, saying the only way to a pleasant afterlife is through them, otherwise you suffer in a horrible place like Hades."

Julian smirked as he filled a goblet with wine and took a sip. "I don't understand it, either," he said, plucking a grape from a dish and eating it. "That's why I took the time to study the *Torah* and the *Gospels* and write about it. My hopes are that people today and forever can hear my call for sanity, especially amid these harmful scriptures that boast of flimsy fabrications and ludicrous lies that even a blind infant would deny."

Paine looked on with anticipation and trepidation, knowing that he only had fifteen minutes, and he truly wanted to hear more of Julian's views on religion before he woke up.

Meanwhile, Julian continued, "Right from the start, the Hebrew god, Yahweh, denied his love and support for every person that walked His planet, except for the one tiny tribe he called Hebrews, or simply Jews. Tell me, Salutius, how could an all-powerful god of all Creation make such an intolerant and singular pact with a disenchanted lot like them? A small tribe of wanderers, who have rarely ever held a parcel of land for any significant length of time, and have suffered one calamity after another, with locusts and floods, or tragedies like their poor fellow called Job. And to top it off, they have been enslaved by one regime after another, century after century."

Salutius nodded. "To my knowledge, it seems they have always been enslaved, by many; the Egyptians, then the Assyrians, then the Medes, then the Persians...by Jove! I've lost count. And now we ourselves are their overlords."

"What's most troubling," Julian continued, "is that their god placed all his love and attention solely on them. Yet, what have the Hebrews really contributed to civilization? Other than the grandest illusion?"

Salutius sniggered. "Yes, not much."

"Not much indeed," Julian said, as he started to pace back and forth as he orated. "Yet look at what the unchosen, or *heretics*, I believe they call us, have accomplished: The Babylonians and Hellenes offered the world studies on the heavenly bodies. Geometry was given to the world by the idol-worshipping Egyptians, arithmetic started with the Phoenician merchants, philosophy was cultivated in Greece, Hippocrates was the father of medicine, and of course, we Romans have given the world the greatest Code of Laws ever conceived, a republican form of government with three bodies of administration and our imperial alteration, huge marketplaces, colossal arenas, baths for the public's cleanliness and enjoyment, the Circus Maximus for entertainment, the creation of the *vigiles urbani*, to fight fires and protect our citizens from crime, and a wealth of literary texts that forgo the illusions of false gods and offer serious historical works by great authors like Pliny, Tacitus, Livy, Suetonius, or works by great leaders, such as Julius Caesar, philosophy by Marcus Aurelius, humorous plays for entertainment, epic poems by Virgil or Ovid, and in total, a great abundance of excellence." Julian stopped pacing and shook his head, annoyed that the masses couldn't see the obvious.

Meanwhile, Salutius listened with rapt attention, as did Paine, as Julian resumed his lecture. "And here's another point about this Hebrew god, Salutius. He is constantly hailed and worshipped for his devastating acts of vengeance and wrath, wiping out entire cities with brimstone and fire or deadly locusts, or inflicting heretics with boils or famine, or Moses' sister with leprosy. Moreover, he killed 70,000 of his own chosen Israelites with a plague, simply because King David took a census, which their god viewed as being prideful and not having trust in him. And as for their god's very nature, he clearly states in the *Torah* that he is a very angry god who demands that his flock fears him, that they slaughter animals to his exact specifications for rituals, prohibits them from eating certain meats, why, I truly don't understand, demands all men get circumcised, again, a very odd request, and he boasts of being a very jealous god. And woe to them who dare think of another god; out comes his arsenal of plagues, famines and hideous diseases."

Julian stopped pacing and looked directly into Salutius's eyes, and queried, "Mankind, in every other religion or cult, has been wisely groomed to imitate those of great character, morals and success, which naturally included their gods. So tell me, Salutius, does this Hebrew god sound like someone you would strive to emulate?"

Salutius sighed. "As *they* would say, *Dear Lord, no!* Never! Especially after all that you've wisely revealed."

"I'm pleased to hear that, Salutius," Julian said. "And as for the rebel Jew called Jesus. His very being was clearly refuted by Moses, who said there was 'only *one* god, and there is none else beside him.' Yet Jesus' disciple Matthew foolishly tried to fit him into their scriptures by tracing his bloodline back to David via Solomon, which listed twenty-eight generations. Meanwhile, in direct conflict, Luke traced it back to David via Nathan, thus listing forty-three generations. Basically, the Jesus tribe had little, and contradictory, knowledge about Jesus' true heredity."

Julian shook his head in disbelief at their erroneous efforts, as he continued, "Worse yet, they lacked any sense of logic, as they claimed that Jesus was born by his mother having been impregnated by the Hebrew god, which instantly negates the bloodline connection to his mortal stepfather, Joseph, whom they also call his father, for some ironic reason. I truly believe that these Jews, who lived in lands rich with opium poppies, were drunk with delusions when they invented these bizarre stories. Yet, what I also find quite ironic is that these Christians are deeply repulsed and appalled by Zeus and other gods for impregnating mortals, yet when their god impregnates a mortal woman to give birth to their Jesus, it is somehow so miraculous and beautiful as to be like nothing the world had ever seen or was lucky enough to be graced by." Julian huffed, exasperated, and added, "Their illogical ineptitude and hilarious hypocrisy is mindboggling. Yet far worse than these delirious authors are the mindless fools who believe this nonsense."

Salutius almost burst out with laughter, but restrained it to a chuckle. "These chosen Jews and Jesus fanatics make it all quite clear. They're *all* crazy!"

Just then Paine's vision went black! His mind grunted with disappointment at the abrupt termination, as his eyes slowly opened. Once again, Ernest stood by his bedside with a glass of water. Paine shook his head, which throbbed even more on this second journey.

Ernest handed him the glass. "So, how did it go?"

Paine took a large gulp and then wiped his mouth with his hand. He paused a moment to collect his thoughts, then said, "Ernest, it ended t-too soon, b-but I must s-say, this was beyond my expectations. To be right t-there when critical m-moments in history happen is s-something that...well, it's hard to explain."

"Did you manage to gather the information you needed for your book?"

Despite his throbbing headache, Paine smiled. "Indeed I have. As I mentioned, m-much of Julian's works were intentionally destroyed, lost, or possibly hidden by Catholic bishops." His face turned sour. "Unfortunately, I'm faced with the s-same dilemma."

"What's that?"

"I wish I could c-change history, because I know the exact date of my visit. It was June 25, 363 AD."

Ernest flinched. "How could you be so precise?"

Paine looked at Vérité with solemn eyes. "Because the n-next day Julian rode into battle and was struck with a spear. He died three days later."

Vérité didn't know much about Julian, but by his friend's bout of sadness, he said, "I'm sorry to hear that, Thomas. But we discussed the perils of trying to alter history. There's no telling what would have transpired if Julian lived a full life."

"Yes, I know t-that, too, would only open up speculation," Paine said. "But the human mind has a habit of always dreaming up alternate scenarios. Just like how we stop before making big decisions in life, trying to access which path will bring greater rewards." He took another gulp of water and rubbed his head. He glanced at Ernest. "Actually, my speech has gotten better much quicker this time. However, one thing you can seriously try to alter with this potion is eliminating these headaches."

"Note taken," Vérité said. "I didn't take the potion in such quick succession like you, Thomas. I gave it time to get purged out of my system. Perhaps you should wait another day or two?"

Paine shook his head and took a deep breath. "No, I can't wait. I've been waiting for too many months in this damn prison, getting sicker by the day, and getting no help from my friends, whom I must now presume are my enemies. And I must finish my second part of *The Age of Reason* before I—"

"Don't say it!" Ernest scolded. "Don't lose hope. Now that I'm free, I will do whatever I can to speak to these barbaric officials to secure your release and at least get you medical attention."

Paine's gaunt face and frail sickly body didn't give Ernst much to go on, but he had to offer words of encouragement. It was the least he could do.

"You're an earnest friend, Ernest. Earnestly!" Paine quipped.

Vérité managed to chuckle. "That's it, Thomas. As I always say, 'Levity ensures longevity.'"

"I like that, I just might plagiarize it one day. If I live long enough," he said with a giggle. "But enough of this chit-chat, please hand me the third and last vial."

With reservations, Ernest handed the last and larger vial to his sickly friend. "I truly wish this tonic was something to cure your sickness, Thomas, rather than a joyride into the past."

"Well, I don't know how much joy I'll get, since these time visions seem to offer thrills tainted with regrets. But, I'm on a quest for knowledge and enlightenment, so joy is secondary. Yet, there is joy in the abstract sense of what this potion offers mankind. This will prove to be a great learning tool, and I foresee great things to come."

"I hope so, too. Well, bon voyage, Thomas," Ernest said with gratitude and compassion. "And remember, this journey will be a bit longer in duration."

With that, Paine swallowed the potion and, once again, his mind beheld a spectral light show, when suddenly a startling vision materialized.

Gusty winds screamed through the chiseled chasms of the Judean desert, as Titus and his 10th legion stood at the bottom of a huge dirt and timber ramp. It had taken his soldiers several months to build it in order to reach the top of the huge mountain, where the Masada fortress sat perched atop its enormous plateau. Inside was where a Sicarii tribe of Jewish rebels had fled to, along with all their women and children.

Paine was in awe, as he likewise stood in this barren wasteland where only this one edifice rose out of the desert, looking like a towering Valhalla. He was well aware of the Masada story, and knew that the Sicarii had made numerous raids and violent attacks on Romans, inflaming the ire of Vespasian, who ordered his son Titus to quash the rebels.

Titus called out to his leading commander, "Flavius, it's time to smoke out the enemy!"

Flavius Silva responded quickly and ordered the soldiers to set the timber they had stacked on fire. Soon, a billow of thick black smoke rose up. But to his chagrin, it headed back down the ramp toward the Romans.

Flavius cowered, expecting a reprimand for the debacle, when suddenly the winds changed and the dense black smoke rose up toward the fortress.

Flavius sighed with relief, as Titus called out, "As you can see, men, this providential change of wind is a sign of divine intervention. The gods are on our side, and these vicious murderers shall learn, once and for all, that anarchy and rebellion are not tolerated in Rome!"

Yet, as Paine looked on with anticipation, the flames and smoke, after twenty minutes, eventually dwindled and proved ineffective.

Growing impatient, Titus approached Flavius. "I cannot tolerate anymore setbacks, Flavius. More importantly, as you can see, the gods had favored a move. Gather the infantry and make a decisive charge up the ramp.

And by the gods, turn this damn rock into rubble if necessary!"

"Yes, sir!" Flavius barked.

With a quicksilver relay of the command, the soldiers strapped on their *lorica segmentata*, then grasped their gladius' and large protective *scutums*.

Flavius and the infantry stormed up the ramp, as their clattering armor and stomping feet echoed throughout the valley. A dry dust arose in the warriors' wake, as their battle cries reverberated among the valley's chasms.

Eager to be a part of the advance, Paine also ran up the ramp, staying close to Flavius.

As they approached the peak, their echoes gradually subsided, giving way to an eerie silence. Like armored beetles, a few soldiers quietly scaled Masada's huge stoned wall. As they reached the crest, they cautiously crawled on their bellies, then peered down, one by one.

One quickly spun around and cried, "Commander, come here at once! You must take a look at this."

Flavius eagerly began scaling the wall, as two soldiers extended their arms down and hoisted him upward. Unsheathing his gladius, Flavius then crawled beside his comrades and peered down.

Flavius' eyes widened as he sprung to his feet. "Mars be damned! What is this?"

One soldier angrily snarled, "I don't know, Commander. But Mars robbed me of filleting these savages."

"Me, too!" another soldier balked. "Those barbarians had killed my brother. By the gods, vengeance should have been mine!"

Then in a flurry of bewilderment, the soldiers sounded off in a cacophony of curiosity.

"Did they starve?"

"Could be, we almost did ourselves while building that damn ramp."

"No, look closer!" another yelled, "They all have been slain!"

One soldier squinted as he tried to focus on the distant bodies below. "You're right! Look at all that blood!"

"I don't get it," another replied, as he stood up, baffled.

Flavius slid his pristine gladius back into his scabbard, and then signaled for his remaining unit to approach. He then turned back toward the bloody carnage below. "Well, I'm guessing they didn't have the rations for such a long siege, but it looks like they killed each other, or possibly even themselves."

"Themselves? But, isn't that against their strange cult, Commander?"

"I believe so," Flavius replied. "I'm fairly certain they're prohibited from committing *desperata salus* (noble suicide). But whatever happened, it certainly looks like their one and only God has forsaken them."

One by one, they crawled down into the huge stronghold and opened the gate for the rest of the infantry to enter. Paine followed. He knew the story, so he expected to see dead bodies. However, actually seeing the carnage was a visceral image he found hard to stomach.

Slowly, the Romans tread through a field of cadavers, gazing at the self-slaughter in disbelief. Over nine hundred carcasses of men, women, and children lay strewn about, coldly drenched in their own languid pools of blood. As they walked past the stiff bodies of women and children, with fresh lacerations through their chests and slit throats, some soldiers became furious, while others turned in disgust. Paine likewise found it extremely hard to look at. He now felt like Dante being escorted through Hell by Virgil.

Meanwhile, other soldiers rummaged through the storage chambers and spotted piles of ample rations, thus dispelling the notion that the Sicarii had run out of food. Along the way they also came across magazines of weapons, and even religious artifacts. To their left was a huge golden menorah, and deep into the far corner was a wooden platform. Two soldiers approached the suspicious grating, as the older of the two, named Antonius, kicked it with his foot.

The younger soldier, Lucas, inquired, "What do you suppose it is?"

"I don't know," Antonius replied. "Perhaps they stored munitions or perishables on it, or maybe performed religious ceremonies here; who knows?"

Lucas smiled. "Well, I know what it's good for!"

Dropping his *scutum*, Lucas quickly grasped the huge menorah and jumped onto the platform. In a juvenile romp, Lucas did a madcap victory dance, while he callously bobbed the massive menorah over his head.

Antonius rolled his eyes and didn't wish to encourage him, but quite unexpectedly, Lucas slipped. As the menorah rammed Lucas on the head, sending him to his knees, Antonius burst out laughing. "That's what you get for fooling around with a sacred artifact."

Even Paine chuckled, finding the cloddy youth's punishment somewhat humorous, since the written histories about Masada never documented such minor and foolish details, not to mention being disrespectful to the Jew's holy relic.

Meanwhile, soldiers in the distance shook their heads disparagingly, as even they didn't appreciate the boy's insensitivity to other people's religious objects.

But then Antonius turned his head sideways and stopped laughing. "Wait! Did you hear that hollow sound?"

"No," Lucas replied, as he got up and continued his mindless dance. "What hollow sound?"

"Never mind! It probably was your hollow head you damned fool. Get down! I want to see what's underneath this grating."

With a perplexed look, Lucas lowered the wobbling candelabrum and hobbled off the platform. They each grasped opposite ends of the wooden grating and began lifting. Overcome with curiosity, other soldiers entered the chamber and huddled around them.

As Antonius and Lucas flipped over the bulky grating, their eyes widened. There, before them, was a hole, approximately eight feet in diameter.

Antonius peered down. What he saw startled him, as several dirty faces emerged out of the darkness, looking like trapped animals in a pit. Two women started to climb upward, followed by five children. Antonius and Lucas each extended a hand to help the women up, as the children quickly crawled out and clung onto their mothers' soiled tunics.

The women began babbling in Hebrew, as Antonius and Lucas indecisively looked at one another. With a rudimentary understanding of Hebrew, Antonius intently listened to their wrenching story. Meanwhile, he discreetly waved to Lucas to summon Flavius.

As Antonius strained to comprehend their words, it was only moments when Lucas returned with Flavius close behind. Brushing the soldiers and Lucas aside, Flavius boldly approached Antonius from behind and stared at the survivors. The women were still imparting their tales of woe, when Flavius demandingly interrupted, "What is this? Who are they, and how is it that they're the only ones alive?"

Antonius turned and faced Flavius. "Commander, they also were part of the Sicarii tribe. And this woman told me that Eleazar, their leader, instructed them to commit suicide. But they disobeyed and managed to sneak off in order to hide. She said at first the tribe refused to comply, but Eleazar's persuasive words slowly cajoled them." Antonius squinted, baffled. "Can you believe it? They did this to their loved ones and then themselves."

Flavius' face twisted with disgust as he grumbled, "What a bizarre lot! By the gods, what were they thinking?"

Antonius stood mute and innocently shrugged his shoulders, while Flavius slowly turned and gazed at all the carnage outside the chamber door. Quickly, he turned back toward Antonius. "Look at all the slain women and children out there. Do you mean to say these warriors actually did this to their own wives and children, and then themselves?"

"Yes, Commander, at least that's what she told me."

Flavius gazed at the two women. "Well, why did they refuse to be slain or kill themselves?"

With a puzzled look, Antonius replied, "Commander, they mentioned something about fearing a Sixth Commandment." Then pointing down at the hole, he added, "So, they sought refuge in this pit."

Flavius looked down into the dark bunker, then back up at Antonius. Pensively he rubbed his chin. "What is this Sixth Commandment?"

Antonius shrugged his shoulders. "I don't really know, but perhaps it's a tribal law of some kind. Should I ask them?"

Flavius paused, then shook his head. "Never mind. Obviously, this commandment can't be too commanding if they disobeyed it. Besides, any tribe that is heartless enough to kill their own family and then themselves doesn't interest me. Extend my congratulations to these women and children for making a wise decision. Then let's gather our gear, and whatever rations or plunder you find here, and report back to Titus."

Many of the soldiers looked at one another and shrugged their shoulders in bewilderment. Paine, seeing the self-massacre with his own eyes, also found it repulsive and hard to fathom. Meanwhile, the soldiers all turned and began rummaging throughout the fortress. As soldiers stepped over dead bodies, some stopped to search through the cadavers' pockets or strip them of jewelry. Others overturned barrels and ceramic jars, and then packed their satchels with dried herbs and other edibles for the long journey home.

Meanwhile, Lucas and Antonius walked straight over to the large golden menorah. They bent over to admire the large decorative candelabrum, then hoisted it up together. Several soldiers drifted nearby to get a glimpse of the impressive trophy, as did Paine, who inspected the fine workmanship. Then they all began to descend the ramp.

Halfway down, Flavius and his troops met up with Titus, who was now marching feverishly up toward them. Paine anxiously moved into position to get a firsthand view.

Titus looked up, and barked, "By Jove, what in blazes is going on? I didn't order a retreat!"

Flavius came to a halt. "*Legatus* Titus, this is not a retreat. Actually, I'm not sure how to explain this, but…"

Flavius did his best to relay the odd and harrowing event, as Paine also listened. After which, Titus heatedly shook his head. He then ordered Flavius to bring the women captives to the frontline.

As the women and children appeared before him, Titus' eyebrows pinched downward. Filled with curiosity, he turned and addressed one of the women in her Hebrew tongue. "So, what has given you impetus to defy your leader Eleazar?"

The woman looked up at the broad-shouldered leader, trembling, as her lower lip quivered. "*Legatus* Titus, when Eleazar commanded our warriors to massacre their kin and then themselves, we knew at once God's will no longer flowed from his lips. And we—"

"*Subsisto! Satis!*" Titus interrupted. Realizing his intuitive Latin outburst, Titus immediately reverted to Hebrew. "How could he, or anyone, accomplish such an outlandish command? What on earth did Eleazar *actually* say?"

The woman nervously paused to gain her composure. Then quite mysteriously, her eyes rolled up into her head as she stood in an almost trance-like state.

Solemnly, she incanted, "My fine memory is a gift of the Lord, and the words of Eleazar are etched in my mind, for he said, 'God has convinced us that our hopes were in vain, by bringing such distress upon us in the desperate state we are now in, and which is beyond all our expectations; for the nature of this fortress, which was in itself unconquerable, has not proved a means of our deliverance. And even while we have still great abundance of food, and a great quantity of arms, and other necessaries more than we want, we are openly deprived by God himself of all hope of deliverance.'"

Then, as if awakened from her trance, the woman's eyes rolled downward and fixated upon Titus, as she continued, "It was then that Eleazar proceeded to sway our tribe. For he conveyed unto them the covenant as a reminder, that hitherto, only we Jews are entitled to the grace of Yahweh. Hence, all those outside the fortress' walls are wicked, and shall fall, like stone, to their graves. For this self-sacrificial deed, Yahweh would honor his chosen. It was then that our tribe bowed to his will. Yet, bemused my sister and I were, until we pondered this act of sin and desperation; and alas, it was one not to be found in our written laws, given to Moses by God himself. As such, it was one not to be fulfilled."

Titus rolled his eyes and shook his head. "It befuddles me how few of you have a grasp of logic. Only seven, among a thousand, placed reason above blind obstinacy. Ever since my father, Vespasian, was a general under Nero, up to his ultimate rise to emperor, of which I soon shall follow, has my family been forced to engage you Jews in this senseless feud. Have we not allowed you the land to build your temples? Do we not permit you to worship freely? Have we not built marketplaces to provide you with nourishment and goods for trade?"

As the woman stood petrified and mute, Titus continued, "How is it that when my father was honored with the title of emperor, even foreign nations sent embassies to congratulate him, yet you ungrateful wretches decided to plot a revolt instead? Do you not see that only a small fraction of Rome's many legions are required to manage your limited numbers? Can you not see that no other nation would be foolhardy enough to embrace your cause, especially against the might of Rome? You arrogant lot, who prosper from our resources, while staying unto yourselves, only to spurn or denigrate us and others who are *not chosen*, and this, all the while under the protection of Rome's mighty sword and good graces. Is it your perpetual desire to shun assimilation, and fight the hand that provides and protects?"

Paine was mesmerized and enlightened by Titus' gripping speech, as he intently listened.

With trembling lips, the woman summoned the courage to utter, "*Legatus* Titus, to speak boldly, our tribe despised your master, Nero, with great passion, and with good reason. He was a wicked man, even by Roman standards, as all of Rome celebrated his death and tore down his Golden House. And Eleazar believed you and your father to be of the same vile blood."

Titus sniggered. "Well, my lady, my Flavian lineage is the first to break free of the Julio-Claudian bloodline. So we quite literally share no blood with our predecessors. Moreover, my father despised Nero, and has every intention of turning this empire back to the Golden Age, which Augustus had miraculously established. Quite sadly, most of his descendants, except for Claudius, failed to follow his noble precedent. Yet, Augustus created the mightiest, most civilized, and most religiously tolerant empire the world has ever known."

The woman's tense shoulders lowered, taking some solace in Titus' words, but replied, "Of your new bloodline's deeds, time will tell, *Legatus*. But you must know, our religion dictates that we follow no authority but that of our own Lord God."

Titus crossed his muscular arms and gazed into her eyes with profound curiosity. "And what did your Lord God say to you atop that monolithic altar—that your own despotic leader, Herod, built ages ago and almost touches the heavens itself? Did he tell your tribe to fight valiantly to defend not only their honor, but more importantly, *His* honor as well?"

The woman stood silent as her shoulders wilted.

Titus shook his head. "Ah, yes, there is no need for an answer. Is there? Eleazar's oration, and the final conclusion, both speak for themselves."

Impulsively, Titus turned toward his troops. "My fellow Romans, you see before you the end result of what happens to rebels who choose not to respect Roman law, or assimilate into our rich culture. Radical nonconformists have no place in civilization, and shall perish by the sword, or as you see here today, ill fortune. Divine providence continues to shine upon us, while a dark shroud shall vex these bands of terrorists until they realize the errors of their ways. We offered them freedom of religion, they chose ingratitude; we offered them free trade, they chose treachery; we offered them protection, and they chose rebellion."

The soldiers began to cheer, as Titus continued, "You see before you a tribe that despises us for making mistakes, as if they are pure and flawless. Yet they even defiled their own religion to become terrorists, using their daggers to kill innocent Romans in public squares, and as you see here today, even ignored their god's rules to commit suicide."

As the soldiers simmered, with eyes glued to Titus' commanding presence and rousing oration, Titus continued, "Or perhaps they despise us for our greatness out of pure jealousy and rage. After all, they learned those toxic traits from their Lord God. It is fine for them to build temples and control their flock, yet they grow bitter at Rome's colossal might that robs them of their rank. Yet, all Rome sought was modest tribute, which in turn gave them free passage to our commerce and culture, and of course unmatched security. Yes, the security to practice their cult unmolested by outside invaders. For Roman law had been the most accommodating to the Jewish sect, more so than any other cult—allowing them to prohibit even Romans from entering their holy temples. Make no mistake, in the final analysis, these wretched souls of Masada chose resignation, we inspiration. They chose destruction, we construction. They chose cowardice, we courage. They chose death, we life!"

The troops broke out into a hysterical roar of jubilation as Titus yelled, "Once again, my brethren, Rome is victorious!"

The troops rallied around Lucas and Antonius and lifted the huge menorah above their heads. Triumphantly, they paraded their trophy down the ramp, shouting repeatedly, "Victoria! Victoria!..."

Paine's vision started to flicker. Then to his chagrin, went black. Slowly his eyes opened. There, before him, stood Ernest, as usual, with a glass of water.

Paine sat up, once again, disappointed that the dream ended, but also elated. After a brief few seconds, he excitedly grasped the glass, and exclaimed, "Dear me, Ernest! That was truly an intense moment. Titus was one heck of a man. He offered so much insight into the perspective of the Romans." Being so excited, he took a gulp of water and started talking before he even fully swallowed. "To view history as it happened, without being revised and manipulated, is truly eye-opening. The Judeo-Christian view of the Masada event has been one of the barbaric Romans hunting down poor Jewish rebels, who took their own lives at Masada rather than submit to the oppressive Romans. That was all a revisionist lie!"

"I do vaguely recall tidbits of the Masada event," Ernest replied. "But, as we know, Thomas, history is often written by those who are victorious. And when the Roman Empire fell, who took control of it? The Christians."

"Yes, and we suffered the Dark Ages because of that," Paine moaned. "The organized Roman machine of government, laws, and economic prosperity collapsed, as small and fractured Christian feudal states arose. And they lost all of the Romans' knowledge of engineering, trade with foreign lands, and state security. Raids by the Vikings easily pilfered, raped and slaughtered many of these feudal states for centuries. They even burned many monastic communities down to the ground. That was the gift of having a theocracy for almost a millennium by Christians. Some victors *they* were."

"Well, you're talking to the choir here, Thomas," Ernest said as he took off his glasses and cleaned them with his handkerchief. "But certainly my devout mother, and countless millions of pious Christians, would have some type of rebuttal for you. Although I'm not sure what that could possibly be after the truisms you and I know."

Paine sniggered. "I'm well aware of what devout Christians would say. They'd claim that Christianity gave Western civilization morals."

"Well, but perhaps that *is* a piece of solid ground they can stand on," Ernest said, placing his spectacles back on.

Paine's shoulders wilted in disappointment, grieved over the misinformed minds of the majority of mankind. "And that, too, is what most people believe, Ernest, even many atheists, like you, unfortunately. And that's because most people don't realize how important learning history is, for there are countless ancient texts by men like Cato or Cicero and others who lived well before Christianity and posited benevolent words of ethics and morals."

Paine closed his eyes briefly; searching his prodigious memory, then said, "Such as when Cicero declared: 'Nothing is more noble, nothing more venerable than fidelity. Faithfulness and truth are the most sacred excellences and endowments of the human mind.'

Or this by Cato: 'I prefer to do right and get no thanks, rather than to do wrong and receive no punishment.'"

Paine crossed his arms and paused, realizing that his speech and headaches were clear, as being passionate about a topic fueled the mind and purged the ill effects. Moreover, he was pleased to have offered Ernest such edifying quotes. "So, what do you think about *those* virtuous words?"

Ernest was genuinely taken aback, feeling like a schoolboy stunned by his mentor's startling revelation. "Very hallowed indeed," he said as he digested his surprise. He then muttered contemplatively, "And yes, that is true, they both *did* live before Jesus and Christianity."

"That they did, my good fellow," Paine said. "So the belief that only through Christianity, or religion in general, can we learn morals is a pure hogwash."

"I am impressed," Ernest said. "I'd even say shocked. But perhaps embarrassed is more apropos. I, like most, have been raised to believe that all pagans, especially before the arrival of Jesus, were barbarians of a sort. And my mother always lectured me about praying and being a good Christian, as that was the only source in this wicked world to obtain morals."

Paine frowned. "Yes, all children of Judeo/Christian families are inculcated to believe their propaganda. And to think, the mighty Christian enterprise has condemned all pagans, including the millions of brilliant minds, like Cicero, Cato, Plato, Aristotle, Thales, Archimedes, Hippocrates, Socrates and countless others, excluding them from God's grace and access to Heaven, just because they were born before Jesus. For Jesus said, the only way to heaven was through *him*. So millions of pagans, including those brilliant men, were never even given a chance, just because they were born at the wrong time. And let's not forget how the entire eastern hemisphere were also left in the dark about Jesus' ministry and likewise were refused his blessings and access to Heaven. So who really are the heathens, Ernest?"

Just then a guard opened the door and peered in. "Monsieur Paine, I have mail for you."

"Thank you," Paine replied, eager to see if there was any good news." He scurried over and received the envelopes, as the guard duly exited.

Ernest sat at the table as Paine paced the dank room and tore open the envelope bearing the seal of the U.S. government. He unfolded the letter and held his breath as he started to read. Ernest anxiously stared as his friend's face went from nervous anticipation to a grin.

Paine's eye's widened as he said, "Well, hallelujah! It's about time. Gouverneur Morris has been replaced by James Monroe on Washington's orders."

Ernest squinted. "How is that a good thing? Morris only seemed too happy to make sure you stayed locked up. So why would this Monroe fellow do anything different?"

"Because James Monroe is a very good friend of mine," Paine said with relief. "And he states that he *will*, without exception, secure my release. Moreover, he roundly detested the shameful behavior and utter negligence of Morris, who, get this," Paine said with derision, "just so happened to be targeted by the French government for spying and giving information to the British. Which explains why Washington was instructed to order his replacement." Paine hissed. "I knew Morris was an unethical snake!" He paused, then shook his dark thoughts free. "But, I can't dwell on that heathen, or on Washington's unsavory pact with him to my very detriment. James Monroe is my liberator, and brighter days are near, very near, Ernest. I know it!"

Excited, Ernest sprung to his feet. "That indeed is fantastic news, Thomas! You've been blessed."

Paine was so enamored by the news that at first it didn't register what Ernest said, until his last sentence rang in his ears. Paine looked at Vérité. "Thank you for the good wishes, my dear friend. But coming from an atheist, it's rather interesting that you said I was blessed."

Ernest's smile withered into an expression of self-reflection. "Yes, it is rather odd, isn't it? I suppose it's just a habit."

"Well, of course it is, Ernest. I meant no disrespect. We are all inculcated from birth with traditions, like when we say 'God bless you' when someone sneezes, or saying 'Jesus Christ,' when something goes wrong. It's all been instilled into our lexicon. And those are all due to our Christian upbringing. That's why Kim Lim, a man I met from Japan, never said those expressions. And the billions of people in the Eastern part of the world grew up knowing nothing of Jesus. Which is another flawed aspect of this Jesus myth, that the majority of our world was never even granted the opportunity to learn about him or worship him. What a ludicrous and ungodly plan. Anyhow, we happen to be products of our Western culture, Ernest. Yet, oddly enough, some pagan traits have managed to survive, like when people say 'By Jove,' who was a Roman god, or how Halloween remains a holiday, despite its true origins harkening back to pagan cults."

Paine paused in thought, then added, "And it's interesting, because I'm sure a devout Christian would say I was blessed to hear news of my release, as they believe any good event is blessed by God. However, that I was arrested on their holy day of Christmas Eve, and spent almost a year in prison on bogus charges, and suffered serious health problems, there is total silence, or the hollow refrain of 'I'll pray for you.' Prayers that did absolutely *nothing*!"

Paine shook his head. "But since I don't believe in their false god, no blessings would I receive. I'm a Deist whose god created this magnificent world and universe but does not interfere with the insignificant daily lives of humans, nor is my god jealous or vengeful or even gracious. As such, there are no afflicting evil people with boils or calamity, and no miraculous changes of health or good fortune. Those are all simply part of nature. We are all born of atoms, as are the Earth, Sun, Moon and our vast universe. Mankind is a biological animal, Ernest, and is a member of a colossal biological family of different creatures on Earth. We may sit at the apex of the pyramid regarding intellect, but that high level of intelligence is insulted and degraded by illogical beliefs in superstitious myths."

Ernest nodded thoughtfully as he sat back down. Pensively, he said, "Yes, as a practical chemist I rarely give philosophy and religion much thought. Perhaps I should." A smile reappeared on his face. "But enough of that. I'm truly elated that this Monroe fellow is serious about your release, Thomas. I only hope that France one day has an honest government like the one you and your fellow American's crafted."

"So do I, Ernest," Paine said. On brief reflection, he paused, then said, "Although, despite a fantastic *Declaration of Independence,* crafted by my good friend Thomas Jefferson, I'm deeply appalled that others pressured him to make one very significant revision."

Ernest rubbed his goatee, curious. "And what was that?"

Paine walked over and plopped on the bed. Irritably he looked at Ernest, and said, "He was forced to eliminate his lines regarding the abolition of slavery. After all, his document states that man is created equal and entitled to equal rights. Yet, in America, such is not the case for African slaves. This has long been a matter of great concern to me, being the first in America to write about the atrocity of slavery. And isn't it interesting that it wasn't a priest, pastor or rabbi who spoke out about that. No! It was I, a Deist, the so-called immoral heretic."

He glanced at the floor as the wheels in his mind churned, then looked back up. "Yet, it's odd that many don't even realize that Thomas Jefferson, James Madison, Ethan Allen, and even Ben Franklin are all Deists. Ben, Thomas and Ethan even wrote about their beliefs. But after the backlash by the Superstitious Sentinels of Christianity, they have since kept their beliefs private. I, on the other hand, shall not cower to them or to the lies by which they shackle the masses in darkness. I shall be the light and speak the truth, for standing firm for truth is the only way it will enlighten and free mankind from the grandest of all illusions."

Realizing his tangent, he looked at Ernest and sighed. "Yes, I often get sidetracked by how religion stirs my blood, hence why it's imperative for me to finish my book, *Age of Reason*. Anyhow, regarding not eliminating slavery in America, it will indeed come back to haunt them one day, of that I am most certain."

"And well it should," Ernest said. "It's barbaric and inhumane. And you would think that they'd have no problem abolishing what African slave traders started in the first place."

"Yes, Americans didn't start the slave trade, but indeed they should have ended it. Do you realize that even the Romans offered their slaves freedom?"

Paine explained that the process was called *peculium*, where masters gave their slaves seed money to start businesses. This allowed slaves to learn valuable trades, develop strong work ethics, learn managing skills, and even keep a percentage of the profits. Most importantly, slaves could eventually buy their freedom. This system benefited both masters, by drawing on an additional source of income, and slaves, who could earn solid livings and their freedom.

Ernest stood up, once again feeling like a flunking schoolboy, and grasped his coat. "Well, Thomas, I can truly say that you are an endless font of information, and I'm honored that you're my friend."

As he slipped on his coat, Paine walked over and shook his hand warmly. "And I, too, am honored to have a friend as brilliant as you. I truly hope that you acquire the chemicals and resources you need to continue working on this miraculous potion. As I said, it will truly be the greatest tool for learning ever created. When people can go back and view the actual events of history (without the bias of authors or used as propaganda by governments or religions), it will finally reveal integrity and truth to us all."

EPILOGUE

On November 4, 1794, James Monroe arrived at the Luxembourg Palace prison to collect his good friend. Thomas Paine had been incarcerated for almost a year (having been neglected by Washington and Morris, whose attention had been on reestablishing trade relations with Britain), while also having suffered serious health issues.

In December 1794, Paine was reinstated into the French government's Convention, but he didn't resume activity due to health issues and having returned to his house in New Rochelle, New York to convalesce. The Reign of Terror had claimed more than 40,000 lives, and as Edmund Burke prophetically stated: *The French can not craft a government that can keep control, and this will open the door for a savvy general to unify his military, and that army will obey him and his despotic agenda.*

Hence Burke had foreseen Napoleon's rise and takeover that would soon thrust France and Europe into utter turmoil. Nevertheless, Paine had once again traveled to France, where he met with Napoleon in 1799, before he declared himself emperor. Napoleon praised Paine, by telling him that he slept with a copy of *The Rights of Man* under his pillow, and even stated "a statue of gold should be erected to you in every city in the universe."

However, once Napoleon seized full control, Paine lambasted the emperor, saying that Napoleon was "the foremost charlatan that ever existed!"

On June 6, 1795, Paine was devastated to learn that Ernest was charged with witchcraft and was led to the gallows, while agents burned his laboratory to the ground, along with all his notebooks and resources. His miraculous potion, which Paine believed would ensure mankind's ability to learn the truth, was destroyed.

Heartbroken, Paine uttered, "The superstitious beliefs of fanatical elements of mankind shall never cease until eradicated with *logic* and *common sense*."

THE AUTHOR/ARTIST

Rich DiSilvio is an award-winning author of thrillers, mysteries, historical fiction, Sci-Fi/fantasy, history and children's books. He has also written articles and commentaries for magazines and online resources. His passion for history, art, music, architecture and software development has yielded contributions in each discipline in his professional careers.

DiSilvio's work in the entertainment industry includes projects for historical documentaries, including James Cameron's *The Lost Tomb of Jesus, Killing Hitler, The War Zone* series, *Return to Kirkuk, Operation Valkyrie*, and cable TV shows and films such as *Tracey Ullman's State of the Union, Celebrity Mole, Blood Ties, Monty Python: Almost the Truth*, and many others.

He has written commentaries on the great composers (such as the top-rated Franz Liszt Site), and conceived and designed the *Pantheon of Composers* porcelain collection for the Metropolitan Opera, which also retailed throughout the USA and Europe at major performing arts centers.

His artwork and new media projects have graced the album covers and animated advertisements for numerous super-groups and celebrities, including: Pink Floyd, Yes, The Moody Blues, Cher, Madonna, Jay-Z, Willie Nelson, Miles Davis, the Rolling Stones, Alice Cooper, Black Sabbath, Queen, and many more. Meanwhile, DiSilvio's fine art appears in galleries, magazines, and museums, including those in the USA and even Russia.

As a software designer/developer, Rich pioneered the first interactive software for educating staff and parents about Applied Behavioral Analysis (ABA) for training individuals with autism.

Rich lives in New York with his wife and has four children.

Having previously published five volumes of short stories of various genres, including sci-fi and speculative fantasy, this book follows that trend. However, that it tackles the provocative subjects of religion and politics I felt it needed its own separate title. As always, I am indebted to all those writers and film script authors who have influenced me over many years. From Rod Serling and his spectacular group of writers of the *Twilight Zone*, such a Richard Matheson, Charles Beaumont and Earl Hamner Jr. to Ray Bradbury, Gene Roddenberry, George Lucas, and George R.R. Martin, and the many other authors and historians throughout history, including but not limited to, Cicero, Ovid, Tacitus, Suetonius, Livy, Josephus, and the authors of the *Torah, New Testament* and *Quran* among others. I thank you!

To my steadfast family and friends, and of course my dear readers, who have supported my creative endeavors, along with my editors, marketers, and to all the contest judges who have voted several of my books as award winners, including the Best Book Cover Awards for my artwork and design, I am most grateful.

— *Rich DiSilvio*

My Nazi Nemesis

GOLD AWARD WINNER

★★★★★ "DiSilvio's plot is cunning and ingenious!"
-- *Jack Magnus for Readers' Favorite*

A deadly love triangle launches a father and daughter team to hunt down a nefarious Nazi. Yet twists and turns abound, leading to a shocking climax.

Hardcover: 9780981762586
Paperback: 9780981762579
eBook: 9780981762593

A Blazing Gilded Age

INTERNATIONAL AWARD WINNER AND BEST COVER DESIGN

A riveting rags-to-riches saga about a poor family's struggle to survive amid a nation burning with ambition yet bleeding with injustice. Features, Teddy Roosevelt, JP Morgan, Mark Twain, Tesla and more.

Lauded by HISTORY/A+E and noted biographer Roger DiSilvestro.

Hardcover: 9780981762562
Paperback: 9780981762555
eBook: 9780997680720

Tales of Titans Series

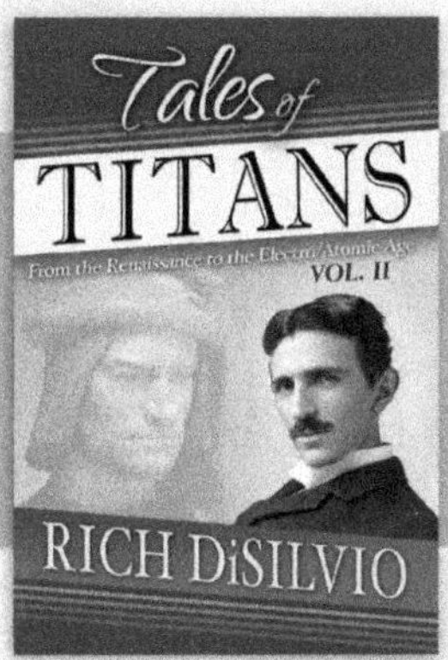

Tales of Titans brings great historical figures to life with concise yet compelling essays, coupled with engaging narratives that enlighten readers to their miraculous deeds, and misdeeds, that have significantly shaped Western civilization.

This handsomely illustrated series offers readers brief biographical overviews and cogent analysis, while the quasi-fictional scenarios transport readers into a fascinating past, whereby putting flesh on the bones of several titans and offering glimpses into their hearts, minds, and actions.

Tales of Titans, Vol. I : From Rome to the Renaissance
Augustus & Livia, Vespasian & Titus, Hadrian, Constantine, Dante, Brunelleschi, Columbus, Vespucci, King Ferdinand, Pope Alexander VI & Cesare Borgia, and Leonardo da Vinci.

Tales of Titans, Vol. II: Renaissance to the Electro/Atomic Age
The Medicis, Gutenberg, Lorenzo de Medici, Savonarola, Leonardo & Machiavelli, Martin Luther, Queen Elizabeth I, Shakespeare, Galileo, Darwin, Marx, Stalin, Freud, Marconi, Edison, Tesla, Westinghouse, Einstein, Fermi and von Braun.

Tales of Titans, Vol. III: Founding Fathers, Women Warriors & WWII
Samuel Adams, Thomas Paine, George Washington, John Adams, Thomas Jefferson, James Madison, Alexander Hamilton, Ben Franklin, Sybil Ludington, James Armistead Lafayette, Elizabeth Cady Stanton, Susan B. Anthony, Harriet Tubman, Adolf Hitler, FDR & Churchill

Liszt's *Dante Symphony*

A historical mystery/thriller highlighting the belligerent rise of Nazi Germany from its Prussian roots, replete with ciphers, spies, murder and a stellar cast, including Albert Einstein, Rossini, Liszt, Nazi officers and Adolf Hitler.

Hardcover: 9780981762548
Paperback: 9780981762531
eBook: 9780997680713

The Winds of Time

The Winds of Time is a historical tour de force of Western civilization by Rich DiSilvio.

With masterful style, DiSilvio paints a fascinating historical canvas with the flare of a consummate artist. Key figures and the primary cultures that literally shaped the Western world are candidly analyzed, revealing both the dark and luminous sides of mankind. Moreover, DiSilvio's insightful essays add intriguing new dimensions to the historical record.

Hardcover: 9780981762524
eBook: 9780997680706

SILVER MEDAL WINNER

Meet My Famous Friends

Inspiring kids with Humor! A whimsical picture book that pays homage to great historical figures in imaginative ways.

Author/Illustrator Rich DiSilvio presents a broad array of geniuses and heroes in a humorous and compelling fashion by altering their names and appearances, whereby making us see very familiar people in very different ways.

While children will get a kick out of looking at the comical artwork, teens and even adults will appreciate the witty play on words, inventive creations, and perhaps glean a thing or two about some of these iconic people who had a great influence on society in one form or another. Their lives and contributions have uplifted humanity in various ways, thus being great role models for young and old alike.

Hardcover: 9780997680751 Paperback: 9780997680768 eBook: 9780997680775

PURPLE DRAGONFLY WINNER

Danny and the DreamWeaver

A MS novelette by Mark Poe (aka Rich DiSilvio) about the power of dreams and the imagination.

When Danny meets Nostrildamus in his dream a bizarre journey begins!

Packed with dry humor, a mystery, and zany-looking artists, like Michelanjello & Hippopotamus Bosch, *Danny and the DreamWeaver* is an imaginative adventure of criminal intrigue and art history that demonstrates the importance of looking at life differently.

Paperback: 9780997680737
eBook: 9780997680744

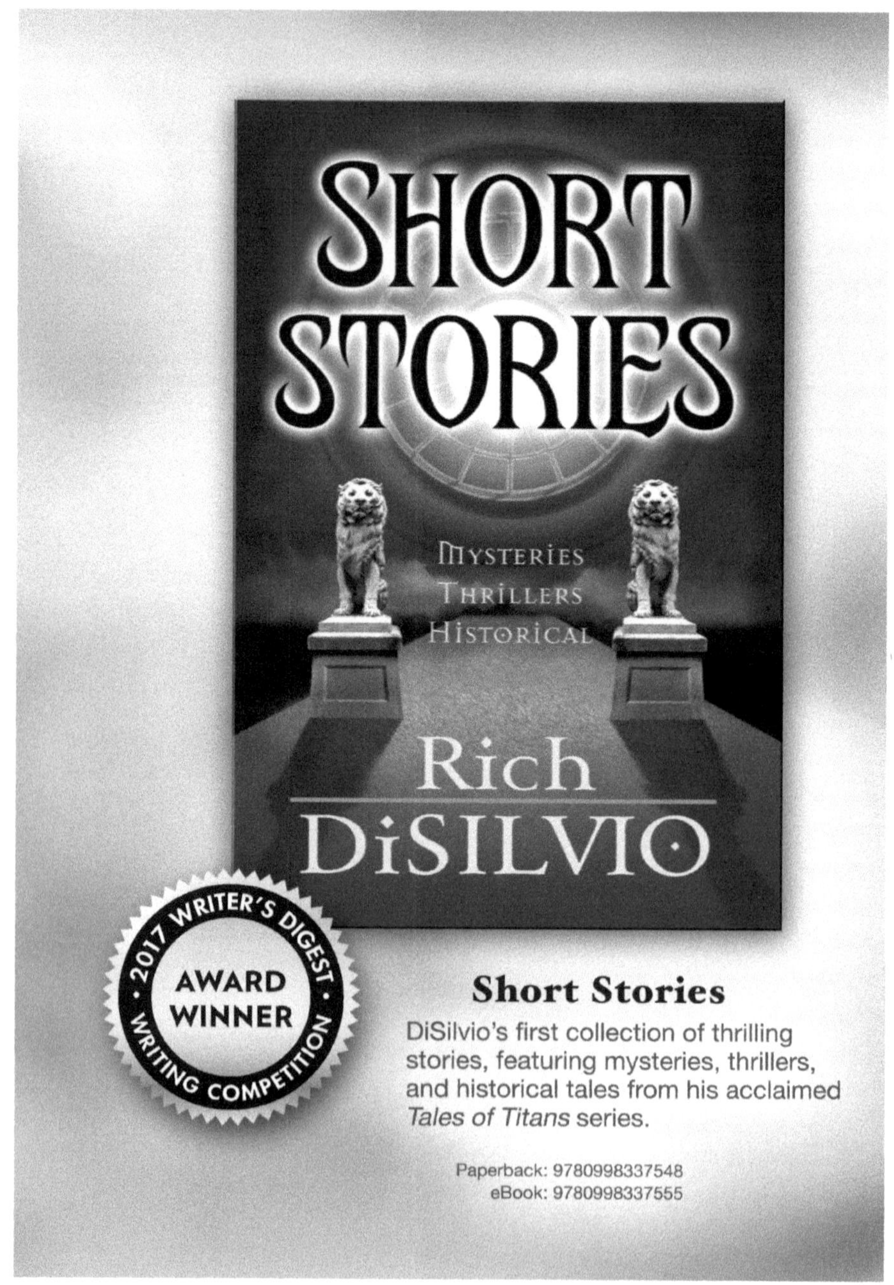

Short Stories

DiSilvio's first collection of thrilling stories, featuring mysteries, thrillers, and historical tales from his acclaimed *Tales of Titans* series.

Paperback: 9780998337548
eBook: 9780998337555

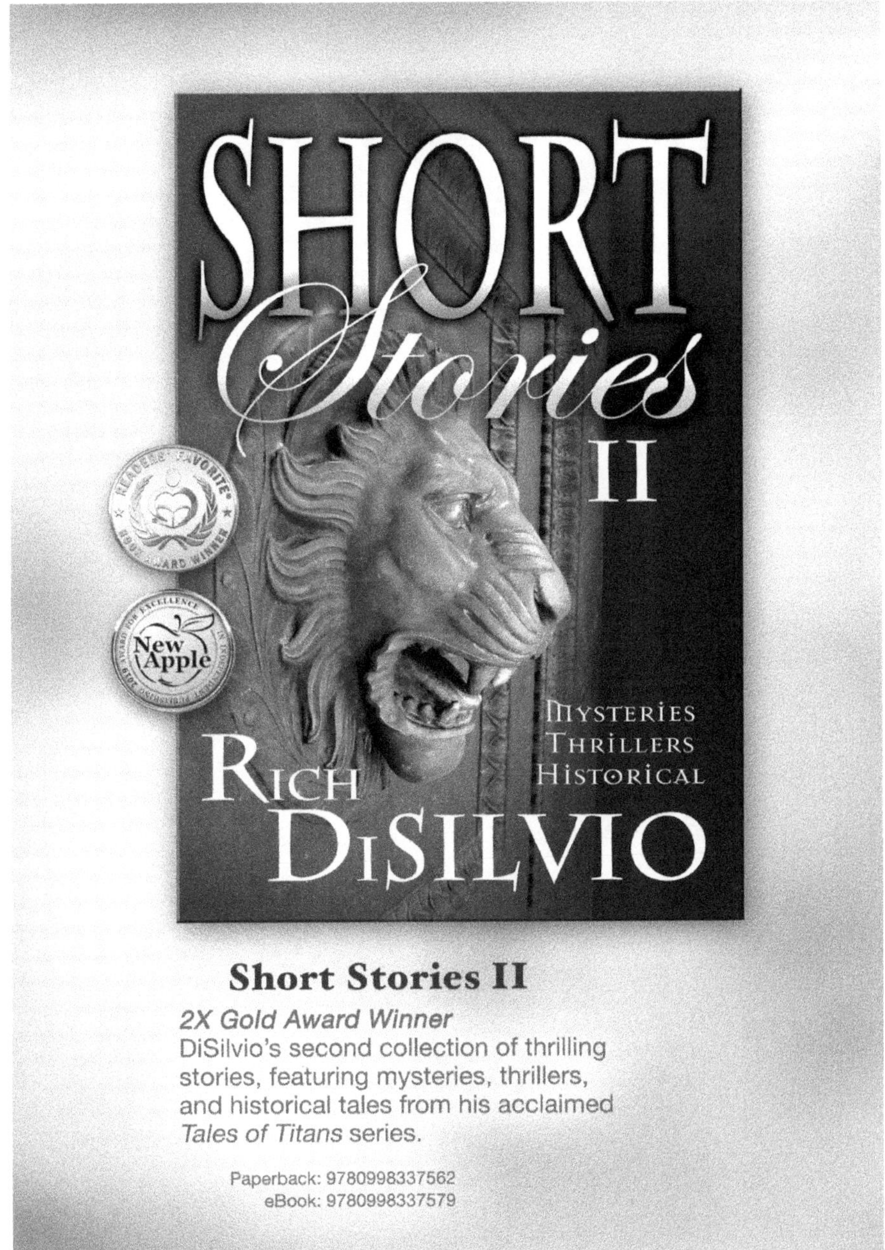

Short Stories II

2X Gold Award Winner
DiSilvio's second collection of thrilling
stories, featuring mysteries, thrillers,
and historical tales from his acclaimed
Tales of Titans series.

Paperback: 9780998337562
eBook: 9780998337579

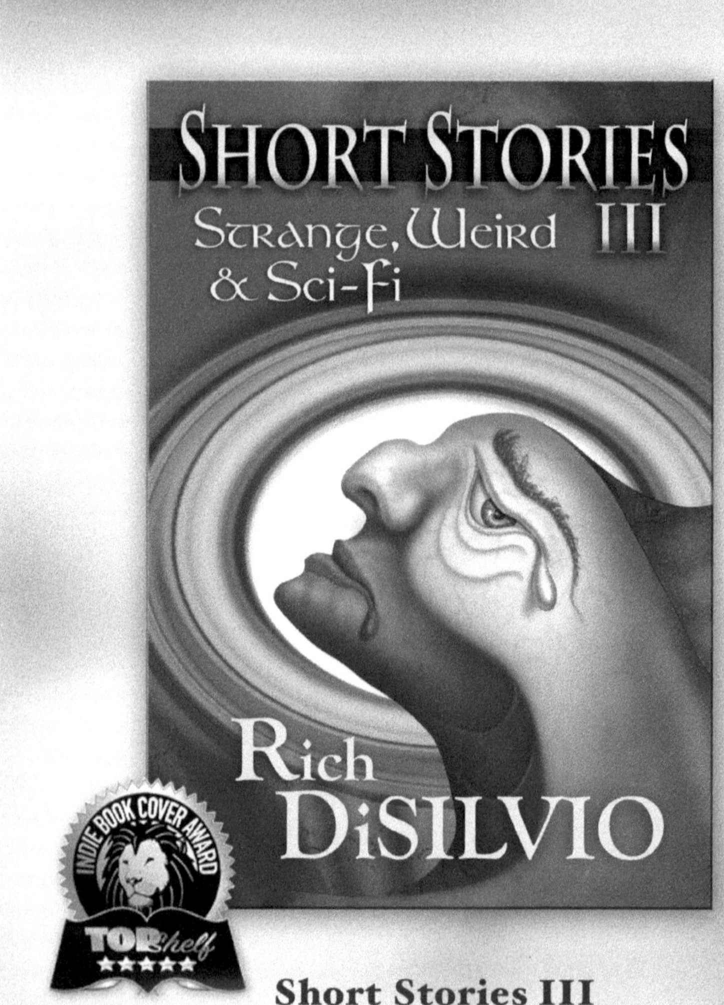

Short Stories III

From the vivid imagination of multi-award-winning author/artist Rich DiSilvio comes this spellbinding collection of fantasy and Sci-Fi tales.

Paperback: 9780998337586
eBook: 9780998337593

Short Stories IV

From the vivid imagination of multi-award-winning author/artist Rich DiSilvio comes this spellbinding second collection of fantasy and Sci-Fi tales.

Paperback: 9781950052004
eBook: 9781950052011

Short Stories V

Lovers of Rod Serling, Ray Bradbury, Isaac Asimov and other icons of the genre will find the vivid imagination of author/artist Rich DiSilvio equally spellbinding in this fifth edition of Speculative Musings.

Paperback: 978-1-950052-08-0
eBook: 978-1-950052-07-3

Leonardo vs Michelangelo

Leonardo and Michelangelo stand as the two premiere geniuses of the Renaissance. Amid personal rivalries, they were also put in direct competition to see who would be the greatest. And although that title is not easy to apply, they did surpass each other in certain fields, hence the need for this critical study.

eBook: 978-1-950052-09-7